W9-BRW-541

2/07

FLiRT
Spin City

By Nicole Clarke

GROSSET & DUNLAP
Published by the Penguin Group
Penguin Group (USA) Inc., 375 Hudson Street,
New York, New York 10014, U.S.A.
Penguin Group (Canada), 90 Eglinton Avenue East,
Suite 700, Toronto, Ontario, Canada M4P 2Y3
(a division of Pearson Penguin Canada Inc.)
Penguin Books Ltd, 80 Strand, London WC2R 0RL, England
Penguin Ireland, 25 St Stephen's Green, Dublin 2, Ireland
(a division of Penguin Books Ltd)
Penguin Group (Australia), 250 Camberwell Road,
Camberwell, Victoria 3124, Australia
(a division of Pearson Australia Group Pty Ltd)
Penguin Books India Pvt Ltd, 11 Community
Centre, Panchsheel Park, New Delhi - 110 017, India
Penguin Group (NZ), Cnr Airborne and Rosedale Roads,
Albany, Auckland 1310, New Zealand
(a division of Pearson New Zealand Ltd)
Penguin Books (South Africa) (Pty) Ltd, 24 Sturdee
Avenue, Rosebank, Johannesburg 2196, South Africa

Penguin Books Ltd, Registered Offices:
80 Strand, London WC2R 0RL, England

**Cover and interior design by Michelle Martinez Design, Inc.
Illustrations by Marilena Perilli.**

Library of Congress Cataloging-in-Publication Data

Clarke, Nicole.
 Spin City / by Nicole Clarke.
  p. cm. — (Flirt ; 4)
 Summary: Trying to sample all that New York City has to offer before her internship at *Flirt* magazine ends, sixteen-year-old Kiyoko overdoes it and gets in trouble at work and with her housemother, but help from unexpected sources leads her to her one true passion.
 ISBN 0-448-44123-3 (pbk.)
 [1. Journalism—Fiction. 2. Animation (Cinematography)—Japan—Fiction. 3. Music—Fiction. 4. Fashion—Fiction. 5. Japanese—United States—Fiction. 6. New York (N.Y.)—Fiction.] I. Title. II. Series: Clarke, Nicole. Flirt ; 4.
PZ7.C55433Spi 2006
[Fic]—dc22
                    2005034467

10 9 8 7 6 5 4 3 2 1

FLiRT

Spin City

By Nicole Clarke

Grosset & Dunlap

KIYOKO'S BLOG:

NÃO! I cut off the hood of my raincoat to make a little purse. It was a mistake and I regret it. Far too impractical and rather slippery.

MY FEET. No matter what fashion laws Her Lordship Josephine Bishop wants to impose on her wage slaves, the ankles of Kiyoko Katsuda answer to a higher authority. Gravity is NOT just a good idea! (Besides, JB is a throwback. She threw me into Entertainment and gave Fashion to Liv Bourne-Cecil.)

SO: Wear the combat boots, love the combat boots, and let heads roll!

RUMOR: My number-one fave anime composer, Jiro Kanno, is in New York! Genius! I have all his soundtracks! Must find! Must meet!

MOOD: OPTIMISTIC. I AM KIYOKO!

MUSIC: THRASH METAL, THE MUSIC OF ANXIETY!

chapter one

It was Monday morning, Kiyoko Katsuda was fresh and at her desk, and there was so much to do.

Hmm, I really need to redesign my avatar, Kiyoko thought as she studied the winking anime face blowing kisses beside her most recent blog entry. Kiyoko had created her avatar during a stretch of downtime—call it loft restriction last Saturday for missing curfew again. Mini-Kiyoko had long black hair, enormous almond-shaped eyes, and wore a kamikaze-style headband that read *Manga me!* She was wearing clothes identical to Kiyoko's current outfit: a vintage *Rose of Versailles* T-shirt and a purple miniskirt made out of sari material. Her name, KIYoKO!!!, flashed down the right side of the little square in Broadway lights.

The only problem was, the parts taken as a whole weren't distinctive enough. The icons she had created for her three Flirtmates—Mel, Alexa, and Liv—were far cuter than her own.

Maybe I'll go back into the feline family. Use a tiger or something. After all, I am Kiyoko K-A-T-suda.

She poised her hands over the keyboard, listening to the crazed thrash metal blaring down the corridor. It was so loud, it was making her desk vibrate. She hadn't been kidding about the anxiety. Something was up with her boss, Trey Narkisian, and had been for about the last two weeks. She bet that if she could check out his blog, it would read MOOD: SCREAMING ON THE INSIDE, YELLING ON THE OUTSIDE. If screaming and yelling could be considered a mood. There were circles under his lovely, lovely blue eyes,

> ## " She was sixteen, in New York for the summer on a Flirt internship … "

and his gaunt-cheek look was no longer aggressively metro; it was aggressively sleepless and fritzed out. And there seemed to be no way to cheer him up.

The trashy thrash segued to Motörhead, which was equally frenetic but not as angry. Kiyoko liked it better, but it was still not reggae, which was much more conducive to her serenity. She missed that sliver of inner peace: The crazed members of the Entertainment division here maintained their frenzied trajectory, rushing, working, working harder, and jockeying for position as top wild and creative worker bees. Not that she had a problem with that. She was sixteen, in New York for the summer on a *Flirt* internship, and she lived in an actual loft with actual other very cool girls from all over the world! Life was good!

And in the Entertainment division, life was always conducted with a soundtrack. The thrash was affecting her fellow proletarians: Caitlain, one of the associate editors, was shimmying down the hall in jeans and a slinky top with a big black notebook and a tower of CDs cradled against her chest. In the next cubicle over, Liss, who spent most of her days organizing book, movie, and food reviews, was drumming on her desk while she talked into her headset.

Phones rang. People loped up and down the halls.

Working in Entertainment reminded Kiyoko of being in a casino. Bright, noisy, frenetic, fun.

The cute new copy-editor guy named Jer stuck his head into Liss's office, yakked a sec, and ticked his glance toward Kiyoko. When he saw that she was looking back, he broke into a heavenly smile and gave her a jaunty wave. She waved back. *Ka-zoing!* He was so totally into her.

Then Liss motioned to her screen, and Jer returned to his regularly scheduled conversation. Liss nodded to the music as she talked to him, then took a phone call; Jer left with one more wave for Kiyoko. She pointed her forefingers at him—*You got it goin' on, baby!*—and watched Liss type very, very fast as she talked on the phone.

That woman is so busy, Kiyoko thought. *I'd better finish my redesign and then do something interny.*

Gazing off into space as she ran through possible looks for her icon, her entire system went on a red alert as—

Aiya! I have been transported to the realm of the hotties!

Shawn the mail guy hunched over his mail cart and pushed it along the corridor. His perfectly chiseled chest and shoulders were in a dark blue T-shirt that did so very, very much for his hazel eyes and sandy, spiky hair. The bloke needed to be in a fashion layout in *Flirt.* She mentally started putting some pages together, imagining him in a tux, in a suit, in a Speedo . . .

As if he could sense her lustful vibe, he grinned at

her. Unabashed and unapologetic, Kiyoko grinned back. He pantomimed looking through the mail for something for her. She pantomimed ripping it open with her teeth. His brows raised and he started digging for real through the stacks like a madman.

Over her laughter, her phone rang. She lifted the mic to her lips—she was wearing the headset upside down like a stethoscope—and said, "How may I entertain you?"

"I'm returning Trey's call," said a voice.

"One moment, puh-lese," Kiyoko answered in a nasal staccato. She buzzed her boss. "Master Trey-sir," she said, "you have a call."

"Who is it?" No "Hi, Kiyoko, how you doing, Kiyoko?" like in the old days.

"Ah." Her gaze ticked back toward Shawn, who waved at her and moved on. She waved absently back.

"Kiyoko?" Trey snapped.

"I . . . I'm sorry. I didn't ask," she replied, closing her eyes and wincing. "But they are returning your call. So it must be someone you want to talk to, don't you think?"

There was a moment of silence. Then he sighed. "Find out who it is."

Her second line beeped as a red light flashed on her sleek black phone console, which she had decorated with *Shonen Jump* stickers.

"There's another call," she told him, meaning that she had to put him on hold.

"Then answer it." Ouch. Ouch, ouch, ouch.

"That was my plan," she said, forcing cheeriness where none existed. "So I'll—"

The red light went out. Caller Number Two had disconnected.

"I'll answer it," she said faintly.

She went back to the first caller. "May I ask who's calling?"

"Yes, of course. It's Janet's publicist."

Janet? *Janet Jackson?* Oh, dear heavenly planets, who *else* went by "Janet"?

Kiyoko took a breath. "Hold on, please. I happen to have Trey on the other line."

She switched over. "Trey? It's Janet's publicist," she said excitedly.

"Janet who?"

An IM flashed on Kiyoko's screen, catching her attention. It was Alexa, asking her if she wanted to go to Nobu for dinner. Kiyoko's busy brain multitasked. Alexa must have snagged another printable photo of someone *Flirt* wanted. Nobu was expensive and the Flirtatious Four only went there for special occasions.

"Janet . . . I thought it must be Janet Jackson," Kiyoko admitted to Trey. "Hold on."

She went back to her original caller. "May I ask what you would like? And also, who you are, exactly?"

"What? *He* called *us*! Are you a temp?"

Insult! Kiyoko wrinkled her nose and caught her lower lip between her teeth. "I'm so sorry, I . . ."

Line two flashed back on, followed by line three. Kiyoko returned to Trey. "They won't tell me."

"You need to find out," Trey said.

"Um, she's getting kind of irritable," Kiyoko ventured. "She said that you called them."

Silence. Sigh. Then Trey said, "Put her through."

Kiyoko went back to the publicist. "Mr. Narkisian is on the other line," she announced.

"I *know* that—"

"So I'm transferring you to his private, direct line," she finished cheerfully. "Have a nice day."

Before Janet's person could say another word, Kiyoko pressed the black button next to the red button and—

No! Press the white button!

Disconnected her.

"No!" she cried, jabbing buttons—red ones, white ones, black ones, any ones. "Come back!"

The dial tone buzzed in her ear like a wasp.

She buried her head in her hands. What a pure and utter blunder. What a disaster.

The phone rang again.

"'Yes!' she cried, clinging to her headset as if it were delivering oxygen and she were a thousand feet beneath the surface.

"Yes!" she cried, clinging to her headset as if it were delivering oxygen and she were a thousand feet beneath the surface.

"This is Consuelo at the lot," a woman said. "Does Trey still want the water tank?"

"I . . ." *Think, lad, think. Do this one right.* "I'll find out and get back to you." She picked up a gel pen and her custom-made "While You Were Abducted by Aliens" notepad, created especially for Trey, and said, "Does he know which lot this is? Will he know which water tank?"

"Yes. My, you're efficient."

"Oh, dear God, thank you," Kiyoko blurted, so delighted by the compliment that she gave her invisible caller an air kiss. "May I have your number in the unlikely event that we don't already have it?"

The woman chuckled and gave it to her. "Tell him we need to know by eight at the latest."

"I will," Kiyoko promised. "Thanks for ringing us up."

Consuelo disconnected. Meanwhile, whoever had been on line three had also given up. She sat for a moment staring at the phone console with all its colorful anime stickers, begging Janet's publicist to call back. Did she need to tell Trey about this? She screwed up her face, less than ecstatic at the thought. The bloke was *so* cranky . . .

To her right, Liss motioned to her through the glass wall and plastered a handwritten sign against it. It read *Sushi order. U in?*

Yum! Kiyoko nodded. She pressed her hands to her sides and undulated back and forth, opening and closing her mouth and bugging out her eyes.

Liss cracked up. On the other side of the paper she wrote: *Eel?*

"Bingo!" Kiyoko cried, with a big thumbs-up.

Then Liss's smile faded. She put down the paper, turned back to her monitor, and started typing like a madwoman.

Confused, Kiyoko cocked her head, trying to get Liss's attention, but Liss steadfastly ignored her; and Kiyoko immediately realized that whoever had freaked out Liss had to be standing behind *her.*

Fixing her mouth in a bright smile, Kiyoko said, "'ello, mate," in a thick Cockney accent as she turned in her swivel chair.

The face of Ms. Josephine Bishop, the CEO and publisher of *Flirt* magazine, glowered down at her like the big head in *Motor City Senjuku Seven.* In the case of the anime show, the head was a friend. In this case . . . Kiyoko didn't think so. Bishop's painted-on hair and her dark lipstick were in place, but her trademark cold, surgical smile was nowhere to be seen.

Kiyoko had never expected to see Bishop in her humble cubicle, and she was mesmerized, like a little mouse facing a rattlesnake on the verge of sending it to mouse heaven. Elegant in a black silk blouse and simple A-line skirt that *had* to be St. John, Top Diva oozed wealth, elegance, and power.

News anchors and movie stars courted her. She'd been to the White House many times; she hung out with queens and duchesses and sultanas; and she did business with kings, dukes, and sheiks.

"Ms. Katsuda?" Bishop queried, crossing her arms over her chest. "What are you doing?"

"Working," Kiyoko announced with a very big smile. She tossed her hair and said, all cutely, "How about you, Ms. Bishop?"

Her überboss's Botoxed lips parted. Then she blinked. Quite a feat, with that lid tuck. But Kiyoko instantly saw that she had miscalculated—Bishop obviously didn't get that she had been joking. The temperature in the cubicle seemed to drop about ten degrees. Kiyoko had the sudden conviction that there was a trap door beneath her chair and that with one snap of her fingers, Bishop would send her down to the dungeons reserved for those who failed to amuse her.

She crossed to Kiyoko's side and peered at her computer screen. Kiyoko did, too, with one eye. *Erk*. Mel had joined the IM party:

Mel_H: KiKo? Nobu?

But Kiyoko instantly saw that she had miscalculated—Bishop obviously didn't get that she had been joking.

"You're working," Ms. Bishop said in the frosty vocal stylings of one who has spent her entire life in an igloo.

Kiyoko gestured to her headset. "Phones," she said, unwilling to go down without a fight. And in truth, she was doing a pretty good job. One disconnection per day was allowed, was it not? "Consuelo at the lot. The water tank."

Another long, cold winter of silence. Maybe Bishop stood there for two seconds, maybe five years. Kiyoko's foot—her bare foot, because her retro Catwoman stilettos had given her blisters—tapped against the carpet. As discreetly as she could, she pushed her hand on her thigh to stop it and pulled both her feet underneath her chair.

Finally Kiyoko could stand it no longer. She said, "Is there something you wanted, Ms. Bishop? Can I get you something? Do something?"

The phone rang.

Kiyoko hesitated, gazing up at Bishop, who gestured with her perfect French manicure for her to take the call.

Kiyoko pounced.

"Good morning, *Flirt* Entertainment," she said in her best secretary voice. "How may I help you?"

"Did you hang up on me?" It was Janet's publicist!

"No, well, yes," Kiyoko answered helpfully, avoiding Bishop's eyes. "And sorry about that, may I put you through now?"

"What's your name?" the caller demanded.

Blast! Kiyoko was about to tell her when Bishop swept back out of the cubicle and continued her royal progress down the corridor . . . toward Trey's office.

"I am so, so sorry," Kiyoko said into the phone, letting a thick Portuguese-Japanese accent flood her voice. "I am an intern here in America, and I'm trying so very hard, please forgive." Kiyoko's father was a Japanese diplomat, so they traveled a lot. She grew up in Brazil, spent several years in Tokyo, and just as many years in London.

"Just get me Trey," the caller snapped. And then, a little less harshly, she added, "Janet's breathing down my neck."

Kiyoko understood in that moment that she was dealing with a minion, like herself, and that this person might possibly be having a rotten day because she was failing to meet her boss's unreasonable expectations. *I so get that.* With a rueful chuckle, Kiyoko said, "These *people.* My God."

"Just get me Trey."

"On it," Kiyoko promised snappily. She buzzed Trey again.

"What?" He was talking through clenched teeth. Kiyoko could tell, because he had been doing it more and more often.

"Hey, Trey, I'm sorry for the delay." She paused, marveling briefly at the rhyme she had just created. "The Janet person is back on the line."

"Can't talk right now. Take a message."

She closed her eyes. "Trey, I'm so sorry, but—"

He sighed. She hated these sighs. She wanted to say

to him, "Lighten up, mate! Nothing on earth is that dire!"
But she did not.

She just waited.

"Put her through, Kiyoko." It sounded exactly like
"Turn in your badge, Kiyoko."

She said, "On it," and deftly, perfectly, expertly put
the caller through.

This called for a celebration. She scribbled on her
"While You Were Abducted" notepad and held it up to the
glass wall on Liss's side. It read: *Also, fatty tuna sashimi.*

Liss glanced her way, nodded, and managed a weak
smile. She looked like she had gas.

Then she IMed Kiyoko.

```
Liss_T: What did Bishop want?
Kiyoko_K: Fashion advice!
Liss_T: LOLOL!
Kiyoko_K: It's all good! :)
```

Kiyoko waved at Liss to reassure her. Blimey, everyone
was so jammed up. Had it always been this way at *Flirt*, and
she had just not noticed? Was something going on that no
one had told her about? She was actually beginning to feel a
little nervous herself . . .

Wait, no, I am not! Everything in my *reality field is
shatteringly fine.*

She smiled to herself and turned back to her desk.

Shawn the dashing young mail guy appeared in the

doorway. He said, "Hey."

"It's for horses," Kiyoko shot back, and they both cracked up.

Shawn glanced left and right and took a furtive step into her little phone-box office.

"Listen, Kiyoko," he began, his cute cheeks pinkening.

He has it so bad. "Yes, lad?"

"Are you guys allowed to date?"

Snap! It was always nice to be asked; and no worries, she was good at letting guys down easily.

"Alas," she began, "maybe my fellow interns are allowed, but I have a boyfriend."

Matteo was her green-eyed American hunk boyfriend, snagged at the International School in Tokyo last term. She called him her *tomo-boyu,* which did not actually mean anything in Japanese. It was something Kiyoko had invented to describe her so-sweet-but-very-long-distance guy.

"Oh." Shawn looked surprised. Kiyoko was just the merest trifle miffed. "Okay." He smiled at her. "My loss."

"It is," she said with great sincerity, and they both cracked up again.

"Well, if you change your mind, you know where to find me." He made a show of taking a giant step backward into the corridor.

"I do, on Mondays through Fridays," she replied.

He swept back down the corridor to reunite with

his mail cart. Their exchange reminded her that she hadn't texted Matteo in, oh, at least twelve hours, and it was definitely time to do so. She picked up the hood of her raincoat and pulled out her Razr, pausing at her wallet, where her most treasured possession in all the world lay.

She said, "Matteo," and the sucker began to dial him, when her *Flirt* phone rang.

"Rats," she muttered, tempted to ignore it. Then she saw that her caller was none other than Trey.

In one easy, graceful motion, Kiyoko dropped the Razr into her hood-purse and punched Trey, so to speak.

"Yessir," she said, touching the mic on her headset to make absolutely sure that he could hear her properly.

"Kiyoko."

"Yes."

"Don't *ever* give me calls from 'Janet's publicist' again."

He hung up.

She sat stupefied. *Okay, what just happened?* As her foot tapped the carpet, she tried to reparse the chain of events: Janet's person called; he said okay; Kiyoko disconnected her; then he said—

Her Trey line rang again.

"Yes," she said hesitantly.

"Lynn just called. You sent the wrong JPEG."

Kiyoko's eyes widened. Lynn was Alexa's boss in Photography. Last Friday, Trey had told Kiyoko to send her a JPEG of Reese Witherspoon for a feature they were doing.

And she had sent it right away. *Vavoom!* Over to Photog!

"I . . . did?" She was flummoxed.

"Yeah. You did."

"Oh."

Trey sighed *again.* "Look. You're probably aware that something's up."

"I am," she confirmed. *I am! I was right! Jammed up, the lot!*

"And I need you on my team, Kiyoko. Especially right now."

"I am. I am very much on your team, my liege." She said that last thing to remind him of the old days, when they would joke and josh together.

"Good. Get back to Lynn."

He disconnected, and Kiyoko realized those days were over. Or on hiatus. Or had been a figment of her imagination.

Perplexed about the incorrect file, Kiyoko opened her e-mail account and started scrolling. She got to Trey's message: *Send Lynn RW2-1.jpg.*

Below was her own e-mail to Lynn. *From Trey.* The attachment was labeled RW2-1.jpg. She opened it up and compared it the original RW2-1.jpg, which was in a file on her hard drive.

Same picture. The correct picture.

Now what? She wanted to call Trey back and clear her name, but he was obviously in a mood, and that meant no mood to listen to reason, she supposed. It seemed that every time she spoke to him, that mood got worse.

But I've done nothing wrong!

Trey buzzed her again. "I'm going to have Hilda take over the phones for a while. Ask her for something to do."

Hello? Was she being sent to the showers? She had not come all the way to New York as a *Flirt* intern to slave for Hilda, Trey's executive secretary. Hilda didn't like Kiyoko—Kiyoko had no idea why . . .

"Trey," she blurted. "I sent the correct picture to Lynn. I checked. I sent the one you asked me to send."

"Well, it's the wrong one," he said.

"But I did what you asked," she underlined.

"Are you arguing with me?" His voice was sharp. "Find out which one she wants and send it to her."

"Okay. I will." She nodded eagerly, even though, of course, he couldn't see her. "Right now, before I report to Hilda. Okay?"

"Fine." There was another sigh. "Kiyoko."

She swallowed. "Trey."

"Do you know about *Rustle*?"

"Are you daft?" she cried. Then, "I mean, yes, I do. I know all about *Rustle*." It was all the buzz in all her anime chat rooms and lists. *Rustle* was a cutting-edge anime feature film directed by Shinichiro Matsumoto's rival, Bobby Honda. The brilliant band Lenin Must Be Buried provided the soundtrack.

"Why don't you go see it tonight? There's a show at six. We need a review."

She gasped. "You want *me* to review *Rustle*? You *are* my captain!"

He actually chuckled. "There are four passes."

"I'll take them!"

"Okay. Drop by my office around four."

They hung up, and she let out a whoop. She IMed the others at once.

> Kiyoko_K: Lads! Film? Rustle?
> Alexa_V: Good movie?
> Liv_B-C: 2 tired, but thanx!
> Kiyoko_K: Cutting-edge anime!
> Alexa_V: No, gracias!
> Mel_H: I'm in!
> Kiyoko_K: We'll leave from loft 6 SHARP.
> Mel_H: No Nobu? OK w/U, Alexa?
> Alexa_V: N/P. Another time, sí?
> Kiyoko_K: Sí. Who did U snap?
> Alexa_V: BRAD PITT!
> Kiyoko_K: SHUT UP!

I'll buy her some champagne, Kiyoko thought, extremely pleased for her mate.

Then she punched in Lynn's phone number and got to work.

⊙　　⊙　　⊙　　⊙

At four she knocked softly on Trey's door. He growled, so she went in. He had an actual office, as opposed to a cubicle like she did. His office was large and very glassy, but he had a couch, *four* chairs, a smashing stainless-steel coffee table, and a matte steel desk that was so large, he could sleep on it if he wanted to.

"Hello, my master," she said. "May I have the *Rustle* passes?"

"Huh? Oh, yeah." He kept staring at his computer screen as he gestured to the corner of his desk. There was a CD for a group called Chaos in Action and four movie passes. She snagged the passes and studied the cover of the CD. Cool-looking guys.

"I straightened out the JPEG thing," she said.

He ticked his glance from his screen to her. "And?"

"Um, it was the file she wanted. The one I sent in the first place." Oops. Meaning that he had been wrong all along . . . and given his mood . . . she was probably not going to become a diplomat, like her father, reminding her boss that he had made a mistake. She smiled hard at him, willing him to see some humor in the situation. "That's so funny, huh?"

He looked at her as if she were speaking in a foreign language, which she could well be, since she was fluent in Portuguese and Japanese, although her grandmother might argue about the Japanese part. She said Kiyoko's accent was atrocious. But grandmothers were like that.

Then he said out of the blue, "I just confirmed an

interview with Geff Wilcox at four thirty at the Silo. I gave it to Liss. You go with her, all right?"

"You are kidding," she blurted. Geff Wilcox was one of the world's most excellent percussionists. To meet him . . . what an enormous coup. To sit in on an interview was incredible good luck.

"And I want you to proof this for me," he continued. "You know I don't like to give you things to do after work, but I'm jammed. These are the Spotteds for the next three issues. You know what those are, right?"

She nodded. "They're little celeb bits that we plant throughout the magazine," she said. He turned back to the screen. "You two better go now," he said without looking at her.

"On it!" she cried, turning on her heel and hurrying back to her sector of the workplace. Liss was already picking up a very nifty black leather satchel. She saw Kiyoko and smiled at her.

Kiyoko dashed into her cubicle and picked up her raincoat hood. She met Liss at the intersection and stepped into pace with her.

"I cannot believe this," Kiyoko confessed. "Geff Wilcox!"

"Believe it," Liss said. "This is the kind of thing that happens when you work for *Flirt*." She exhaled slowly. "I'll miss it."

"What? Are you leaving?"

They headed out of the maze of glass walls and

noise. People sailed all around them. The main receptionist at the entrance to the *Flirt* offices was fielding calls like an octopus.

Liss shook her head as she steered Kiyoko past the woman and toward the lift that would take them to street level. She said in a low voice, "I think I'm getting fired."

"No!" Kiyoko cried. She really liked Liss. "Why would they fire you? Trey's sending you on an important interview! They wouldn't fire someone who's interviewing Geff Wilcox."

Liss signaled her to lower her voice. "It's all crazy here lately, if you haven't noticed. I think some heads are gonna roll. And I think one of them will be mine."

"Then you have to fight to stay," Kiyoko insisted. She smiled encouragingly. "Right?"

"I'm not sure I can," Liss confessed. "This is a very high-pressure environment. Maybe I don't have the stuff."

"You are daft!" Kiyoko cried. Heads turned. Abashed, Kiyoko covered her mouth with both hands. "Sorry," she mumbled.

"Me too." Liss's face was crumbling. She caught herself and smiled grimly. "But not every story has a happy ending, Kiyoko."

That is so defeatist, Kiyoko thought, horrified.

Then the lift arrived, crowded with people, which cut off any further discussion.

chapter two

Chica_snappa: KiKo? Where RU?!
KIYoKO!!!: Alexa! Almost there!
Chica_snappa: Pronto, chica!
   Problema!
>>PICTURE SENT<<

Yikes! *Emma . . . friend. Emma . . . friend,* Kiyoko chanted to herself in the backseat of her cab. Alexa's snap of the *Flirt* interns' resident housemother filled the display of her Razr. Emma Lyric looked grouchy and ready to climb the Empire State Building to bat at airplanes. Which meant not-great things for Kiyoko, who had sworn she would never, ever, ever be late again. But at the tone the time would be . . . she checked her Razr . . . ten fifty-eight! *Aieee!*

In the *Flirt Magazine Summer Intern Program Handbook,* which was about the size of the Tokyo American Yellow Pages, Emma Lyric had been described as "a defacto den mother, someone to turn to for guidance, advice, and information." This reassuring bit of PR was accompanied by a picture of her standing at the entrance of the loft, all smiles and soft lighting. Kind of like Clark's mother on *Smallville:* corn-fed clear skin, jeans, and pinned-up hair. A *Gilmore Girls* ultrayoung mom, whose task it was to guide her sweet-sixteen charges through New York's treacherous waters during their eight-week stay, not devour them like so much sashimi if they were one minute late for curfew.

As anyone who worked in the fashion industry knew, looks could be deceiving. Emma Lyric might resemble someone from one of the FOS—the fly-over states. Maybe she could make a boo-boo face and pass out the Motrin when a girl had cramps, but that chick was a hard-edged New Yorker, handpicked by none other than Josephine "I am *Flirt* magazine" Bishop. A veteran of many summers, Emma had heard all the excuses about being late, and she was buying none of them. Not today, not tomorrow, not on wholesale, not ever.

She had already rejected Kiyoko's argument that the curfew was completely unreasonable because it was impossible to keep. Honestly, who on the shining blue planet could work the Entertainment beat at *Flirt* and still be home in time to catch the eleven o'clock news? With TiVo, maybe . . .

And here was the proof: Kiyoko had gone to the Geff Wilcox interview, which had been brill, then realized she was about to miss the film and hightailed it over there. And then, of course, her hideous mistake—she had forgotten to pick up Mel.

KIYoKO!!!: I'm not late yet!
Chica_snappa: U will B!
KIYoKO!!!: O. thnx. Yoda!

Kiyoko was grateful to the soles of her hideous high heels that Alexa was still talking to her. Kiyoko had not only put the kibosh on the Nobu dinner but had dissed her favorite tofu eater. Halfway through the film she had remembered, so she had dashed into the lobby to call Mel and beg her forgiveness. Which Mel had given her—Mel always would—and en route back into the theater, she had run into none other than Vlad Moscow, lead singer of Lenin Must Be Buried. He was sneaking into the sneak! And of course she had recognized him by his tatts and his piercings and his faboo Bulgarian accent.

"Da, da, I am Vlad," he had confessed.

Coup! Major coup! They sat together to watch the last forty minutes, and then Kiyoko had dragged him to the gelato store next door for an exclusive interview. Thank God she had forgotten to give Liss back her little digital tape recorder, because Kiyoko's batteries had died ten minutes into the interview.

And such an interview! She could see it now:

Flirt: **Some of your chording is reminiscent of the early work of the Rolling Stones. Are you a fan of Ry Cooder?**
Vlad Moscow: Wow, you are really knowing music histories!

Fabulous!

Emma wouldn't care, of course. All Emma would care about was if Kiyoko got home by eleven. Kiyoko had been late more times than everyone else put together. So . . . loft restriction last weekend. All weekend. It had been pure and utter hell.

From the cab, she scanned the rows of illuminated windows on the twelfth floor of her building as it came into view. She had lived with five other girls for six weeks, with two more weeks to go. For Kiyoko that was a personal best. She wasn't positive that she'd lived with her own family for that many consecutive days. The Katsudas were jet-setters, to use an old-fashioned term. Older sister Miko was in London; little bro Hiro was in Tokyo; her mother was on the northernmost island of Hokkaido, taking care of Grandmama; and her father, a diplomat who got to mix it up because the Katsudas were rich, was everywhere.

She checked the time on her Razr. Ten fifty-nine. Curfew in sixty, fifty-nine . . .

She looked at the traffic. Her cabbie was inching along. She could walk faster.

> **Emma wouldn't care, of course. All Emma would care about was if Kiyoko got home by eleven. Kiyoko had been late more times than everyone else put together.**

"Let me out," she told him.

He jerked to the left, triple-stopping in the crush of traffic, and Kiyoko pulled open her hood-purse so she could get her . . .

wallet . . .

My wallet!

She yanked the sides of the hood open from the Velcro tabs she had glued on and felt around inside. She waded through lip gloss, a pen, Liss's digital tape recorder, and more pens; her digital camera; ginger Altoids; several books of matches because although smoking was foul, many of her friends in Europe and Japan still did it; a little pocket guide to all the *Yu-Gi-Oh!* characters; not one, not two, but three half-eaten bars of Toblerone *and* a bag of crisps laden with vinegar and salt; and lots of bits of paper containing e-mail addy's and phone numbers that she really needed to load into her Razr.

Oh, also a light-up pen, some sticks of cinnamon gum, her *Flirt* press pass—pure gold—and a clutch of under-twenty-one bracelets from visits to clubs.

But *no* wallet.

She felt around the seat and swept downward, checking the floor.

As she sat upright, her long black hair covering her face like that evil little girl in *The Ring*, she pushed it away and said, "Don't call the coppers! My wallet is missing, but the doorman loves me. Hold on, he'll pay!"

She waited for him to pop her door. But he was just

staring at her. She said, "Please, I'm going to pay you!" She dug in her purse again.

Aha! She located some singles and a five. Glancing at the meter, then down at the cash, she shrugged and handed him the lot.

The cab door opened.

And it began to rain. Hard.

She didn't care. Dashing through the downpour, she clattered on her stupid shoes through the two other rows of idling or parked cars to the sidewalk, and from there she swam upstream to the corner, where she joined the other five million three hundred and twelve thousand pedestrians surging against the light.

If only I had the raincoat I scalped for this purse, she thought as she maneuvered around the slowpokes. She was getting drenched.

Home free! She blasted through the big green metal door to her building. Her heels clattered on the marble like applause.

"*Komban wa,* wet person," Sammy the adorable doorman said from his bank of consoles, where he usually watched *Lost* and reruns of *Veronica Mars.* She was teaching him Japanese; he said he wanted to learn it, but she knew he just wanted to spend time with her.

"My wallet is missing!" she cried, shaking herself off like a poodle. "My cab driver nearly had me arrested for stiffing him!"

"Oh?" He rose from his console in his maroon

coat and red piping and came over to her. "Is he still out there?"

"No! I found some bills. Popcorn!" She pressed her fingertips across her forehead, then lifted her chin and extended her hand toward the lobby's painted ceiling in a rather operatic pose, which she was self-referentially aware of despite her freak-out. "I paid for the bloody popcorn! *And* the Twizzlers *and* the extra-large diet soda!"

"Emma is waiting for you," Sammy said to her, gesturing for her to get herself to the lift.

"They have one more showing of the film tonight," Kiyoko muttered, whipping out her Razr. Giving him a wave, she started back toward the door, punching in the phone number to the loft. Sammy grimaced and shook his head.

"You should check in with Emma first," he advised her. "She's going to let you have it if you're not up there in . . . twelve seconds ago."

"So doing," Kiyoko informed him, pointing to the cell phone as her call went through. "E-checking in."

He shook his head again.

"Kiyoko?" On the line, Emma was not happy. "You'd better be on the other side of the door that I am opening right now."

"Oh my God, Emma! I'm in the lobby," Kiyoko said. "Nearly outside, actually. I went to the film Trey told me to see, and I left my wallet there. My credit cards, my *stuff*!" A fresh wave of panic washed through her. "I need to go back right now."

"Okay, Kiyoko, try to calm down," Emma said. "Give me the name of the theater. I'll call them and ask them to look in their lost-and-found section. Maybe it dropped on the floor and someone turned it in."

Uh-huh.

"Meanwhile, you stop right where you are and wait for Nick. I'll send him out to go with you."

Every second counted . . . although really, who was she kidding? The chances that someone had turned her wallet in were a big fat zed. This was New York, not Tokyo. Last summer, she had dropped a fully loaded iPod nano in Yoyogi Park and returned to find it nestled on top of its neatly wound headset cord, waiting for its rightful owner.

If something like that happened in Manhattan, it would be on the cover of the *Post*. New Yorkers were not exactly known for random acts of kindness.

"Okay, all right. But please tell him to hurry," Kiyoko begged.

A message was coming in.

SPIDER_K: Hey. KikO! Clubbing 2morrow?
KIYoKO!!!: Hafta C. ok? L8tr?
SPIDER_K: K!

Despite everything, she smiled. Spider K was one of her new New York friends. He worked in the Metropolitan Museum of Art as a restorer, and he had an Icelandic girlfriend who was distantly related to Björk. Apparently everyone in Iceland was distantly related to everyone else. There weren't all that many Icelanders. Spider K had found a brilliant Korean barbecue place that did the delicacies— tongue, liver—all the yummy, scrumptious things that would make someone like Mel send a contribution to PETA.

Mel. Much ado about Mel. What a huge blunder to forget about her.

Sammy returned to his console, saying, "Told you so. You're cutting it too close these days, Katsuda-san."

She said, "You're lucky I'm not mad at you. A friend of a friend is a PA on *Lost*, and he told her what's going on with Sawyer."

He looked so stricken, she almost told him she was lying.

Almost.

Then she turned around as the lift door rumbled open. Emma got out alone. As in, no Nick.

Kiyoko had a bad feeling.

"I called the theater. There's no sign of your wallet," Emma told her by way of greeting. "We should call your credit card company right away. Let's go upstairs and make a list of everything you had in there and what steps you need to take to protect yourself from identity theft."

Kiyoko groaned. Her father was a prominent Japanese diplomat. For some people, snagging his daughter's private information would be the equivalent of hacking into Paris Hilton's Sidekick.

"This is bloody awful," she muttered as she followed Emma back into the lift.

Its door dragged shut like an old man closing a curtain. Kiyoko hoped it wouldn't rebel; she was in no mood to climb twelve flights of stairs.

Emma said, "Well, I'd lecture you on being more careful, but I lost my own wallet last spring. I was the victim of a pickpocket." At Kiyoko's stricken look, she nodded. "I don't know how it happened. I'm usually so careful."

"Me too," Kiyoko muttered.

Emma added gently, "The theater said they'd keep a lookout for it. It may show up. Sometimes people just take the credit cards and money and toss the wallet. Was there anything of sentimental value in it? Pictures of your family?"

"They're all uploaded," Kiyoko said. But there had been a certain fortune-cookie fortune. Matteo had given it to her on their first official date. *You will see the world and charm many hearts.*

"Including mine, Kiko," he had murmured with the hot fuzzies of the smitten. That was their Moment, and the cookie fortune was the symbol. The fortune was tattered and grimy now, but Kiyoko had kept track of that thing the way some people watch their children. It had been her talisman, her mojo, her special thing.

And it was gone.

The lift reached the twelfth floor. The door shimmied once and opened, letting them directly into the Flirt-cave, the huge, airy loft that, had it been Kiyoko's own, would have been hung with the fantastic anime art she had discovered at Quardro's on Fifth Avenue. The dark wood bookshelves of the sunken living room would have been laden with beaucoup windup toys and robots for Matteo. They were sort of geeks in their passions.

"Hello, *Gaucho*," Kiyoko said breezily to Alexa. She didn't like letting people see her off balance, not even the volatile *muchacha* from Argentina. "Funny thing happened on the way home. Lost my wallet."

"Oh my God!" cried Alexa. "*¡Ay, qué lástima!*"

Alexa's dramatic cry summoned the others—Liv, who was perfectly coifed in her cashmere sweats and a Grace Kelly French twist; Gen Bishop, niece of their beneficent dragon lady, in a pair of pajama bottoms and a matching top that said *I Hate Dorks* in Italian (which Kiyoko sort of spoke); and Mel, who appeared at the top of the spiral staircase in an adorable, if threadbare, cotton nightie and flip-flops, grim and unsmiling. Then Gen Jr., aka curly curvy Charlotte, appeared behind Gen, like Paris and Nicole during the good times.

Kiyoko winced when she realized that Mel had glammed up in preparation for her night out with her friend—berry lip gloss, shimmery blush. She'd even done her nails a bright, happy fuchsia. Out with the beeswax lip balm, in with the sophisticate. Kiyoko spared a moment's thought to wonder what Mel had chosen to wear with the look. Certainly not the nightie. Though maybe the flip-flops.

"Hey, Mel, I cannot apologize too much," Kiyoko said, taking a step toward her.

"We did this already. We're good," Mel replied unenthusiastically.

Livid, Alexa crossed her arms over her chest and threw back her ponytail. Her big hoop earrings threw off death-dealing laser beams of reflected light.

"It is *not* good!" she declared. "Kiyoko, you have done this, like, three times in the last week!"

Kiyoko blinked. "I have not."

Alexa extended three fingers. She tapped the first one. "*Primero*. Bagel run yesterday morning. *Segundo*. After work at Nobu last Tuesday to celebrate my picture of Cameron Diaz on page sixty-five. And now this. *La tercera*."

"Bagels . . . ?" Kiyoko was confused. In her world view, not buying bagels together on the way to work was a non-event. They'd see each other, like, ten minutes later at the magazine. So that was really only twice . . . except for number four, which Alexa didn't know about: Kiyoko had failed to connect with Mel at the Starbucks downstairs to discuss whether the girls should get their bosses, Emma, and Ms. Bishop thank-you gifts at the end of summer. Mel had requested a private one-on-one to discuss it. She didn't have much money left, and Miss Moneypants Liv was still trying to pay for Kleenex every time the lad sneezed. And Mel didn't want to discuss it around Alexa without getting clear on protocol, because Alexa was short on cash, too, and she had this habit of going and doing something before she thought it through.

"You've researched New York the most," Mel had told her. "Maybe you'll know what to do."

I already apologized to Mel for that one, Kiyoko thought. But nevertheless, it was another act of evil for those keeping score.

Emma stepped in. "I know this is important, but we need to deal with the wallet."

Kiyoko nodded. "It would probably be best to call my mom in Japan. She's got all my financial information. It's okay to call her now. Really."

"All right," Emma replied. "Why don't you change out of those wet clothes and then come to me."

"Yes, my liege," Kiyoko said.

Kiyoko headed for the bathroom. Mel was no longer in the main area of the loft. Liv, Gen, and Charlotte had drifted away, too, the high drama concluded. *Nothing to see here, folks. Please move it along.*

Loyal Alexa walked with her to their bathroom. Kiyoko popped off her stilettos and wriggled her toes.

Alexa said, "I'm sorry I yelled at you. It's just . . . Mel was so excited to go with you. She read all the reviews. And she waited and waited."

" *But nevertheless, it was another act of evil for those keeping score.* "

That didn't do anything to make Kiyoko feel better.

Kiyoko grimaced. "I probably shouldn't mention this, then, but I met Vlad Moscow. In fact, not only did I meet him, I interviewed him."

Alexa shrugged. "I don't know who he is," she confessed.

"Oh, he's sick. He's going to be an enormous star," Kiyoko said enthusiastically, warming to the subject as she pulled off her *Rose of Versailles* T-shirt and fwopped off her bra. "He was totally into me. He's one of those soulful Eastern Europeans, you know?"

Alexa smiled blankly. "There are some foreign exchange students at my school, but I don't think I've met any Eastern Europeans." She cleared her throat. "You should hurry. Emma was counting the seconds before you called. You don't want to keep her waiting."

Kiyoko frowned. "But I *wasn't* late."

"She said something about pushing things too far," Alexa replied. "Testing the limits."

"I'm sixteen," Kiyoko argued. "I'm supposed to test the limits."

"I hear you, *amiga*. It's too bad you can't go to school with me," Alexa said, her flawless mouth pulling up in a mischievous grin. "You and I could get into some pretty good trouble together."

"Too right," Kiyoko said. Then she pulled down her sari skirt, and they both started cracking up. The cheap material had dyed her thighs purple.

She went to the back of the bathroom door, where she kept her *Spirited Away* bathrobe, and said, "Look, I'm sorry about the bagels. I didn't realize it was a whole thing. You lads should call me on these faux pas. You know me. I'm not about the subtle."

"Okay." Alexa reached over and gave her a quick hug. Kiyoko was not from a family big on the hugging, but it was nice.

"About Mel." Kiyoko glanced in the direction of the bedroom Alexa shared with her, where, presumably, Mel sat in wounded seclusion. "Do you think chocolate would help?"

"It never hurts," Alexa replied with a wink.

They went into the hall. Kiyoko thought about making a quick detour into their bedroom, but Emma was waiting.

"Pray for me," Kiyoko said as they walked to the door of the Lyrics' separate living quarters.

"Bless you, my child," Alexa said, making the sign of the cross in the air. Then she walked away, leaving Kiyoko to face the music alone.

"Emma?" Kiyoko rapped on the door.

"*There* you are," Emma said as she opened the door. She sighed the exact same way Trey had sighed all day, and Kiyoko's anxiety ticked up a notch.

Emma took her into the apartment she shared with her nineteen-year-old son, Nick. It was simply furnished in dark wood and had some nice touches—a plaster alcove featuring a terracotta vase, and a trio of burnt orange candles on the table. The look was understated but by no means shabby-genteel.

And Nick's paintings were everywhere. Several half-finished canvases were arranged on easels and against one wall. The hardwood floor was protected by a tarp and some splotched sheets. Kiyoko loved his vibrant use of primary color and the sense of movement in his work. It reminded her of the energy of anime.

Nick was gone, leaving Emma and Kiyoko alone in the apartment. Kiyoko felt weird around her now. She didn't know what to say, how to act. From what Alexa had said, she was on some kind of probation, and she didn't want to jeopardize her chances of passing.

KIYOKO'S BLOG:

Because I'm officially Japanese—that's what my passport says, anyway—people expect me to be incredibly polite and respectful of authority. But my parents—my father, especially—have taught me to be spontaneous and outspoken. Actually, lots of Japanese kids are like me. Nippon! It's not just chrysanthemums anymore, y'know? Tokyopop comes from TOKYO! We have got it goin' on!

Be that as it may, when I don't meet other people's expectations, I've noticed they're extra hard on me. The other girls have broken the rules just as much as I have, but I'm being singled out.

Or am I just being defensive?

"Here's the phone," Emma said shortly. "Would you like some tea?"

That was really nice. Maybe Emma wasn't as angry as she appeared.

"Thank you," Kiyoko said, smiling at her. It was a smile Emma did not return.

Seated in one of two chocolate brown leather chairs separated by an oval table, Kiyoko phoned her mother. As Kiyoko could have predicted, Atsuko Katsuda was far more concerned about her only daughter than a few stolen credit cards and some cash. Running down the numbers was easy, and Kiyoko's mom told Kiyoko she would take care of it.

The Katsudas chatted for a few more minutes, Kiyoko asking how things were going with her grandmother. Her mother assured her that all was well in hand, but Kiyoko thought she sounded tense and tired. Hokkaido was a weird place. Its major claim to fame was these monkeys who liked to hang out in the natural hot springs. And a big ice festival.

Hiro was going on a trip to Korea with the family he was visiting, and Miko had gotten another modeling assignment. Kiyoko's father was heading a deputation to meet some Chinese dignitaries about trade agreements.

"Me? I'm splendid!" Kiyoko assured her mother when she asked.

After she hung up, Emma returned from the kitchen with two cups of herbal iced tea. Kiyoko knew that was her cue to stay for a Talk. Anxiously, Kiyoko took her cup, which was from MoMA; Emma took a sip out of a *Flirt* cup and said, "So. Things are sorted out about your wallet?"

"No big," Kiyoko assured her. "Thank God."

"Yes." Emma set her cup on the table. "You cut it razor-close tonight, you know."

Kiyoko flashed her a peace sign. "I made it, though, right?"

"Yes, you did." Emma took another sip. "This time. But your life is so . . . frenetic, Kiyoko. You're all over the place. And this isn't the first time you've lost something."

"An umbrella. A sweater," Kiyoko said dismissively. "But it's the first time I lost my *wallet*." A wallet was in a whole different category.

Emma took a sip of tea. And then another. The anxiety was beginning to get to Kiyoko. She was tired and wired, and the air conditioner was turning her into a polar bear.

"These last two weeks are going to be challenging for you girls," Emma said. "You especially. Each intern gets a special assignment, and you haven't had yours yet. And I'm willing to bet that since you're last, they're going to expect more from you. You've had all summer to learn how *Flirt* is put together."

"Has Bishop . . . Ms. Bishop . . . told you that?" Kiyoko asked carefully.

"No," Emma replied. "But Ms. Bishop has discussed her concerns about you with me. She thinks you're not taking your internship seriously."

Especially after her surprise visit today, Kiyoko filled in.

"She is so wrong. I'm working like a madwoman! You know what it's like to be at *Flirt*. A million phone calls, all these things Trey wants me to do. He's so needy." Kiyoko decided not to go there. Or rather, more there. She didn't want to trash him.

"And then there's Bishop . . . I mean, Ms. Bishop . . ." She caught herself. Emma Lyric *worked* for Josephine Bishop. "Almost everything I do 24/7 is linked to my internship."

"Is it too much for you? Please, be honest with me," Emma encouraged her. Her big brown eyes were kind. She was Ma Kent Gilmore, den-mother lady.

"Well . . ." Kiyoko began. And then she caught herself.

Confess failure and weakness to someone who would tell Bishop?

"Yes?" Emma said encouragingly. Her piercing gaze made Kiyoko's nerves jangle.

"No way. It's all good," Kiyoko assured her. "I'm handling all the chaos. I mean, there is no chaos." She dimpled. "English is not my native language, you know."

"It's easy to forget. You're so fluent."

Did you tell Bishop that? Did she mention anything else about me to you?

"All right, then." Emma placed her cup on the table, a signal, perhaps, that their nerve-racking little confab, fun though it had been, was over.

Kiyoko immediately leaped to her feet. "Thank you for the tea and for helping me with my theft."

Emma nodded, rising as well. "You're welcome. Maybe someone will turn your wallet in."

Ya-huh. "Maybe so," Kiyoko agreed. She changed the subject so they wouldn't end on a negative note. "Nick's paintings are brill."

Emma's features softened, the way any proud mother's would.

"Yes, they are, aren't they?"

"He's got a future," Kiyoko predicted. Kiyoko wondered if Bishop was helping Nick make some connections. Come to think of it, the Bourne-Cecils were art dealers. Surely they could pull a few strings for Emma Lyric's kid. Unless that wasn't considered *propah.*

Maybe the Katsudas could help. She'd have to ask her father if there were any Chinese art-gallery people in his meetings.

Unaware of any of Kiyoko's mad thoughts, Emma escorted Kiyoko to her door and said, "Try to get some rest, Kiyoko. Even sixteen-year-olds need some downtime."

"Aye-aye," Kiyoko said breezily, saluting Emma with three fingers like an American Boy Scout.

Emma gave her a look. Kiyoko did not like all these looks. It was as if they were starring in some Kabuki drama, which would inevitably end with someone dying.

Then Emma closed the door, and Kiyoko sagged against the wall and exhaled like a balloon, limp with relief.

I am not in trouble.

Throughout the loft, the lights were off, allowing the shimmering cityscape to sparkle through the windows. She gazed with longing at the Chrysler Building, certain something more interesting was going on inside it. It was maddening to be back inside the gilded cage, looking out at the energy and activity. New York had it going on.

Somewhere out there someone has my wallet, she thought. *And my fortune-cookie fortune from my tomo-boyu, blast them.*

She went up the staircase and breezed directly to Mel and Gen's bedroom; she knocked softly—for her—on the door. Mel and Gen both remained silent when she whispered, "Lads?"

She felt an enormous sense of anticlimax. No Kabuki with Mel tonight. Maybe Mel wasn't all that upset if she had dropped off so fast. She probably had meditation exercises to help with that sort of thing.

Or maybe she was just pretending to be asleep.

Thwarted, Kiyoko went back into the bathroom. Steam from a recent shower moistened the air and frosted the mirrors. Someone had thoughtfully rearranged Kiyoko's

> **It was maddening to be back inside the gilded cage, looking out at the energy and activity. New York had it going on.**

wet clothes over the slats of a wooden clothes-dryer contraption Emma had bought at Crate and Barrel. Since Gen was not thoughtful, Kiyoko figured Alexa or Charlotte had done it. Or maybe sweet Mel, the most considerate of her loftmates. She had probably been raised that way; Kiyoko knew that in Northern California a lot of people lived in communes.

Kiyoko glanced around to see if there were any telltale signs that Mel had been there—if her toothbrush or her favorite herbal hand lotion had been moved, that kind of thing. But nothing was out of place.

Kiyoko began her nightly ritual. She squeezed a dollop of her Shiseido cleanser on her face, leaning forward to examine the bags underneath her eyes. Emma was right. Her candle was blazing at both ends. Truth? It *was* hard to keep up. But it wasn't impossible. Not for Kiyoko Katsuda.

New York is this huge buffet, she thought, brushing her teeth. *There's so much to try. I want to go back for seconds and thirds and fourths and fifths! And I'm almost out of time.*

chapter three

After a quick change into boxers and a tank top featuring Galactic Pirate Ryoko on them, Kiyoko went into the bedroom she shared with Alexa.

In the darkness Alexa murmured, "Everything okay?"

"Yes, lad. Go to sleep," Kiyoko said tenderly as she dropped her purse object beside the bed and rolled onto the mattress, loving her pillow and silky comforter. As her ratty old Picachu—a gift from Matteo—bobbed against her bicep, her muscles groaned in a good way. She had been "on" all day. She hadn't even been able to really enjoy the movie because she'd been busy taking notes for Trey. *Rustle* was totally cutting-edge—from the digitally programmed composition of the scenes to the stylized way the *seiyu* (the voice actors) delivered their lines to how the music was cued to a timing sequence that even Vlad had trouble describing.

And what music! She had sat mesmerized, just listening. She'd closed her eyes and tilted back her head, letting the cascading tonal sequences wash over her like a waterfall. It was like house meets a deep-bass backbeat meets Philip Glass.

She grinned. She *did* know her musical histories.

And now she knew Vlad Moscow.

It had been sheer luck that the rocker had popped in to see how the audience was reacting to *Rustle*. Sad to say, there hadn't been that many people at the opening. Maybe Americans just weren't ready for cutting-edge anime. Give them *Cowboy Bebop* and the latest (wonderful) feature from Miyazaki, and they were done.

He'd sat at the end of her row, which was pretty empty, and she had opened her eyes and glanced over, and nearly fallen out of her seat. She couldn't believe she was watching the movie with Vlad Moscow. Though Vlad had been reluctant to admit who he was, she'd still begged him for an interview.

Which I haven't downloaded yet!

Anxiety prickled the hairs on the back of her neck. She felt in her purse for Liss's digital recorder and pressed it against her ear as she hit the play button, thumbing the volume down.

". . . no, I would not say we are pop band. We are tryink to go beyond labels . . ."

She hit fast-forward and stopped for another spot-check.

"Lenin Must Be Buried have been together for six years . . ."

Good. Everything was still there. She liked his

English. His facility came and went. She knew how that was; sometimes when she was tired or excited, it was harder to think in another language. Someone told her that whatever you used when you counted in your head was your native tongue. That made it Portuguese for her. No wonder Grandmama was so upset.

We are not pop band. She could see that as a header. Maybe a nice shot of him beside the header, and a block of text covered over with a bleed. She loved layering pages, text, headers, subheaders. Lots of information, different platforms—she had made up a name for her own pop-culture journalistic style: Deep Content. She had also tried out PopCult on Trey, which he had informed her was "cute but a little too breezy." She had no idea what he meant, and the best he had come up with to explain it to her was "superficial."

Slow down. Though she was exhausted, her mind was scurrying around like a cute little Japanese badger. Maybe she should plan her article now, because once the day began, she wouldn't have any free time.

She thought about getting out her laptop and checking her e-mail. There was still so much to do!

Tomorrow.

After a lot of tossing, she began to drift off to sleep. The bed was a leaf floating in the wind . . .

And it was then that she remembered that in addition to the popcorn, the Diet Coke, and the Twizzlers, she had also bought the Italian ices. She had insisted on paying for everything because she was interviewing Vlad for the magazine.

Which meant that she had left her wallet *there*!

I'll call them, she thought excitedly. But she couldn't remember the name of the gelato place. No problem: She'd call the theater.

Grabbing her Razr, she bounded out of bed and tiptoed back out of the bedroom. She linked to the Net, got the number for the theater, and called.

She got a recording listing the showings. They were on the last one. Then it hung up. She wasn't going to be able to talk to a real person.

She made a few stabs at gelato places, but none were on the correct street. Just in case, she checked her e-mail. There was a ton of it, but nothing with the header *I Found Your Wallet.*

Then I'll go there, she thought.

Now.

Which could land you in such big trouble.

She tried to be mature about it. The crisis had been handled. Her credit cards were canceled. In the morning, she would have money.

But she didn't have her little fortune-cookie fortune. And the actual wallet had been completely sick, something Miko had sent from a trunk show in London—a black anime demon decorated with black and red beading.

You can ask her to get you another one, Kiyoko reminded herself.

But the cookie fortune . . . that was irreplaceable, just like the credit-card ad said.

Adrenaline dumped into her system as she visualized the joy if she found her wallet. No more lollygagging. She had to give it a shot.

Eagerly, she went back into her bedroom, crossed to the closet, and felt around on her side of it for something to wear. Her fingers closed around the waistband of a pair of capris. She carried them to her dresser drawer and located panties and a bra, and one of several tanks. It didn't matter which one it was. She was not dressing to impress.

She snagged her purse and located her flip-flops.

The light went on. Alexa was sitting up in bed.

"What are you doing, *mami*?" Alexa's ponytail had moved up onto the top of her head, and she hadn't gotten all her eyeliner off so she had black rings under her eyes. Kiyoko thought it looked smashing.

"Please don't say anything," Kiyoko pleaded, dropping her voice to a whisper as she pressed her finger over her mouth. "There was something in that wallet that I have to have. And I remembered that we went to the gelato place next to the theater. It might be there."

Alexa parsed. "So you are sneaking out in the middle of the night to go to a gelato place?"

Kiyoko nodded. "Next to the theater."

"What if it's closed?" Alexa asked.

"It stays open until midnight. Meaning I only have twenty minutes left," she hinted. "If I get a cab right away,

"Kiyoko and El Gaucho, together again! Let the wacky high jinks ensue!"

I can make it!"

"And what about coming back?" Alexa prodded.

"I'll tell the cab to wait," Kiyoko promised. "I'll be super-extra-lux careful. *Te lo juro.* Just don't tell anyone." She mimicked zipping her mouth shut.

Alexa considered. Then she nodded. "Okay. I won't say a word." She paused for dramatic effect, threw back the covers, and added, "As long as you let me go with you!"

Kiyoko smiled wryly. Kiyoko and El Gaucho, together again! Let wacky high jinks ensue! Then she said, "Must give you full disclosure, lad. You know we might get in big trouble."

Alexa moved her shoulders. "Kiyoko, please. This is nothing trouble. This is the kind of trouble amateurs get into. Back home I was legendary for my trouble."

"Point made and taken." Kiyoko smiled at her fondly. "You *are* one for the road trips, aren't you?"

"*Sí, amigita,*" Alexa replied, giving her a little nod.

"In your pajamas?" Kiyoko asked.

Alexa shrugged. She was wearing black-and-red pants and a black T-shirt, which could easily pass for street wear. "I'll put on a sports bra," she suggested.

"Hurry," Kiyoko begged.

Alexa quickly got her chichi sitch handled. But by

then, there was a problem: There were noises coming from the Lyrics' separate apartment. Maybe it was Nick coming home; maybe it was Emma making tea. But it made taking the loft's built-in lift a little more problematic.

"Fire escape," Kiyoko decreed. They'd done it before, and they could do it again.

So they went to the back of the loft and pushed open the little balcony door, letting in steamy heat and traffic noise as they made a break for it.

Looking down twelve stories, Kiyoko thought of every escape movie she had ever seen.

They wound their way down the metal-runged switchbacks, hunkering down in case anyone was looking, and moved from light to shadow and back again. Kiyoko found herself thinking about *Rustle*. There were deliberate, stylized patterns in each scene, like the alternating bars of light-to-shadow-to-light they passed through now.

"*Oye,*" Alexa hissed. "Are you daydreaming? Move faster."

Kiyoko complied, but it was tough. Her muscles were made out of chewy Botan rice candy. She was *tired*.

The last section of the fire escape had been pulled up and secured. Rather than unfasten it, Kiyoko climbed over the side and hung for a moment, then dropped down on her flip-flops into the alley where the Dumpsters were. It stank. There were bits of newspapers and fast-food wrappers on the ground, and some of them stuck to Kiyoko's flip-flops. She was already planning her entry in her blog about how gross it was.

Alexa dropped down beside Kiyoko like Catwoman. She popped back, her ponytail bouncing.

"Wipe under your eyes," Kiyoko murmured. "You look like a zombie. I like it, but others may scream."

"Not one for the makeup," Alexa replied as she did so. "It's just too much work."

Then they tiptoed out of the trash area and hurried down to the opposite end of the block. Cars rushed past, their tires shooting water from the thundershower puddles onto the curb.

Safely out of view of the back window of Emma's apartment, Kiyoko thrust out her hand to hail a cab.

In a matter of seconds, a cab shot over. Twangy Afghani rock blared from the speakers. The dark-haired driver popped the door open and said, "Whereyawannago?"

"The Mondrian Theater on Third," Kiyoko told him.

"Okay." He started the meter, and they were off.

They were sliding back and forth on the seat with each sharp corner he took. The two friends huddled together, giggling and high-fiving each other. They were on a quest!

Now they stood midway between the theater and the gelato place. Kiyoko looked at the red letters set in a yellow background—*Gelato Italia*—and winced. Of course. How could she forget a simple name like that?

There were some white tables and chairs outside, none occupied; inside, beyond more empty chairs and tables, a guy was standing behind the red Formica counter with his back to the girls.

"Say something else," he urged.

Kiyoko was confused. Was he talking to them? She was about to speak when *someone* else replied from around the corner, "No, you are not payink for Vlad's ice cream."

In a very, very familiar voice.

"That's good," counter guy said as he pressed open the cash register and tidied the bills in their little rectangles. "And the chick really bought it?"

Kiyoko's blood iced over. *What?*

"Oh, yeah, way," said the voice. "I didn't have the heart to tell her she had the wrong guy."

"Oh, yeah, *right. That's* why you did it," counter guy said.

Alexa flashed Kiyoko a horrified look. She tugged on Kiyoko's arm, but Kiyoko stood her ground; the toes of her left foot began tapping against the black-and-white checked linoleum floor. She was so angry, she was certain steam was rising from the top of her head.

She had been played!

"Hey." The guy at the counter turned and smiled at them. "What can I get you two lovely ladies?"

Just then, "Vlad Moscow" walked around the corner. He was still wearing the same outfit he had been wearing earlier in the evening—pulled together with a white apron dotted with cherry red, orange orange, and lemon yellow.

And he was carrying a broom.

Kiyoko knew where to put that broom.

His big dark not-Bulgarian-rock-star eyes stared at Kiyoko in obvious recognition and total freak-out. Kiyoko balled her fist, trying to decide which one of his eyes to blacken first.

Alexa caught her arm and said, "Don't do anything crazy, *mi amor*."

Not-Vlad gave her a quirky half smile that was surely meant to charm her and said, "It was all in fun, you know? You thought I was that guy. My girlfriend says I look like him, too."

Your girlfriend?

He had been coming on to her with that stupid fake accent—how could she not have realized just how fake it was, it was the worst in America—*and* he had a girlfriend?

"You pig," she spat out. "You're a jerk, you know that?" Then she extended her arm, making come-hither motions with her fingers. "Give me back my wallet."

Counter guy lost his smile as he looked from Kiyoko to the jerk and back again. Obviously Mr. Ha-ha-ha hadn't shared this part of his fun adventure into deceit and thievery.

"Tommy," counter guy said, "what's this about?"

Vlad—correction, *Tommy*—pulled in his chin and raised his unibrow, extending his arms out to the sides as if he was about to break into song with his broom. Or to protest his innocence.

"Hey, I didn't take no wallet." He frowned at the

counter guy. "Honest."

"You did. You did, and I want my fortune-cookie fortune!" Kiyoko yelled, charging at him like a crazed bull.

Alexa held her back. "*Oye, mami*. Down, girl."

"Hey, hey, hey." Tommy raised his hands. "I'm clean."

"I know you have it. That's why I came back here," Kiyoko said wildly, gazing around. "Give it back or I'll . . . I'll call the coppers!" Kiyoko cried, whipping out her Razr. Which of course she would never do. She and Alexa were here undercover. If Emma or Bishop found out that they had snuck out . . .

"Wait," Tommy said.

Kiyoko glared at Tommy, her finger poised over the keypad.

He was bright red as he said, "Maybe we can talk someplace more privately."

"Why? So your boss won't know he's employing a bloody rotter?"

"Please, miss, just come with me," Tommy begged her.

The politeness of "miss" gave her hope. Unless he was just going to lure her around the corner and bludgeon her.

She handed her phone to Alexa and said, "If I'm not back in *one minute*, make the call."

She didn't say to whom, and Alexa didn't ask. Kiyoko's lovely Argentine sidekick simply nodded very seriously and said, "*Sí, mami. Un minuto,* and then . . ." she waggled the phone in her fist.

Alexa *was* good at trouble.

Boring mental holes in the back of Not-Vlad's skull, Kiyoko trailed him as he left the room and turned the corner into a hallway with a public bathroom on one side and another door marked *Employees Only* on the other.

He led her into an office so tiny that it made her feel smothered, and she wasn't even claustrophobic. There was a little desk made out of fake white wood. On top of a stack of papers, a cheeseburger and fries oozed grease onto a paper plate.

He lifted up the plate, revealing a manila envelope. Not looking at her, he turned it upside down.

Voilà. Kiyoko's wallet.

As thrilled as she was, she was also creeped out. She had never met an actual thief before. Except for herself, and all she had stolen was labeled food in the loft kitchen.

Her face prickled as she darted forward—he had to step back to let her—and snatched it up. With trembling fingers, she opened it.

Credit cards, cash . . .

Her fortune-cookie fortune lay just where she had placed it, stretched across her Japanese high-school ID. Terrible picture, smashing cookie fortune.

The sun would rise in the morning.

"I found it on the street," he said quickly, biting his black-polished fingernail. "I was going to call you to let you know." He hesitated. "But then I didn't. Because then you'd probably figure out I wasn't Vlad Moscow. So I was going to send it to you at *Flirt*. See? It's in an envelope. Honest."

Kiyoko held the wallet tightly in her fist. "That is honestly the best lie you can manage, after you denied having it?" she asked incredulously. "You are a pudding head."

She left him there, stomping back into the gelato store proper, holding her wallet in the air like a flag.

Counter guy was clearly shaken when he saw it. He said, "Oh, my God. He *did* take it?"

"You'd better fire him, mate," Kiyoko told him. "He's probably been nicking coins from your till for centuries."

The guy swallowed. "He's my brother."

"We have a saying in Japan: 'Don't pour water on dead roots.' Come on, Alexa."

They strutted outside like the hot chick pilots in *Gundam Wing*.

"What did you say to him? What did you do?" Alexa had to know.

Kiyoko pointed to her eyes. "Turned him to stone with one glare."

"He deserved worse," Alexa assured her.

"I would have called the coppers, but Bishop and all," Kiyoko said. "So a felon walks free tonight."

"I know. I thought of that, too. That we'd get in trouble if we made a scene. *Ay, te digo,* what a jerk."

Kiyoko was wiping her wallet with the edge of her top.

> ## We have a saying in Japan: 'Don't pour water on dead roots.' Come on, Alexa.

She couldn't stand the idea that he had even touched it.

"He must have gone to see part of the film on his break. He came in late. And I connected the dots, and he decided to have me on." Kiyoko put the wallet in her purse and turned it upside down experimentally. The wallet slid out. Design flaw. "I wonder what his brother will do."

"Maybe his brother knew all along," Alexa said. "Maybe he was just pretending to be shocked for our benefit."

Kiyoko nodded. "Either way, they're rotters. At the very least they could have given us some free gelato."

Alexa nodded, her ponytail reminding Kiyoko of a buoy out at sea.

She dug around in her purse and pulled out one of the half-devoured Toblerone bars. She unwrapped it and broke off a chunk, handing it to Alexa without asking her if she wanted it. Who *wouldn't* want chocolate?

"Salud," she said, touching the rest of the bar to Alexa's before she crammed it into her mouth. It was so enormous, she couldn't close her mouth to chew.

"Taste test. Which do you prefer?"

Alexa took a huge bite and chewed like Kiyoko. "That's a stumper," she admitted. "Why don't you give me some more?"

"Lad, lad, you're an addict," Kiyoko said sadly. "What time is it?"

"Nearly midnight," Alexa replied.

"The last show should be getting out." Kiyoko glanced in the direction of the theater. "You know, in London or Tokyo we'd just be getting started. I'm a night person. Everyone I know is a night person. I can't believe we're in New York and we have to be in so bloody early."

"We do things late in Argentina as well," Alexa said. "I miss midnight supper. And wine with dinner," she added wistfully.

"America, the land of perpetual childhood." Kiyoko dug around in her purse and offered Alexa a stick of cinnamon gum. Alexa took it.

"Well, what's the name of that Shakespeare play?" Kiyoko chomped zestfully. *"All's Well That Ends Well."*

Alexa chomped her gum, too. "But it hasn't ended yet. We still have to sneak back in."

Kiyoko waved her hand like a magic wand.

"We'll be fine." She danced in a half circle. "We'll be singing in the . . . *Oh. My. Nondenominational. God.*" Kiyoko gasped and grabbed Alexa's arm. "Lad . . . look."

Alexa looked.

chapter four

What Kiyoko Saw Outside the Gelato Store That Nearly Stopped Her Heart: Two men were walking out of the theater. Two Japanese men. Two Japanese men whom Kiyoko adored with all her anime-loving soul: the famous anime director Shinichiro Matsumoto, and Kiyoko's number-one idol, his composer, Jiro Kanno. They always worked together.

The tall director sported his trademark lion's mane of stark white hair; the diminutive composer wore a black braid down his back and a Yomiuri Giants baseball cap. They were both wearing baggy cotton pants in neutrals—khaki for Matsumoto and navy blue for Kanno—and leather flip-flops and polo shirts. What men would wear in Japan on a summer night.

Overcome at the sight of her gods—plus having now had a double celebrity sighting in the space of a few hours (even if the first one was a fake), Kiyoko bowed low and called in Japanese, "Good evening, gentlemen."

The two men stopped. Matsumoto-san said in

English, "Did you say something?"

Flustered, Kiyoko couldn't reply in English. She could barely think in Japanese.

The men smiled quizzically, first at each other and then at her, and sauntered toward the girls.

"You are Japanese?" the great director asked, in Japanese. "Do you know us?"

She nodded. "Of course I know who you are!" she replied, also in Japanese. Then she remembered her manners and said, "My friend Alexa speaks Spanish and English." It was the polite way of saying that Alexa *didn't* speak Japanese. Kiyoko was trembling. Her feet seriously wanted to dance.

"This is Shinichiro Matsumoto-san and Jiro Kanno-san," Kiyoko informed Alexa, adding the honorific titles used in Japanese. Not to do so would be like calling someone by their last name only. Like . . . Bishop instead of Ms. Bishop.

"Nice to meet you," Alexa said. She clearly did not know who they were, but she was being very polite. "I am Alexa Veron."

"My pleasure," Matsumoto-san said as both he and Kanno-san bowed to Alexa.

He turned to Kiyoko. "You are an anime fan?"

Talk about your understatement.

"*Hai,*" she said. "Yes. I am a huge fan. The hugest. Of anime in general, yes, but especially of *your* work."

His eyes twinkled. "Not so huge, *ne*?" He gestured to her, pushing his hands inward to indicate her thinness. Famous-Japanese-person humor.

"Please, Matsumoto-san, Kanno-san, may I interview you?" Kiyoko begged. "We're with *Flirt*."

"It's a fashion magazine," Alexa explained, trying to be helpful. "With many interesting articles about music and film."

Matsumoto-san looked dubious. "Excuse me, but you're both very young to be reporters."

"We're interns. Students," Kiyoko amended, trying to save face for him in case he didn't know the word in English. "Oh, I want to ask you so many questions. There's a riot on the *Ghost Hunter Sensei* bulletin board. You killed Tadao!"

Matsumoto-san held out his hands. "Excuse me, please. It was creatively necessary."

"But that meant Kanno-san had to stop using Tadao's melody," Kiyoko continued, indicating his companion. "That was a bloody criminal act."

The director smiled. "Ah? You like Jiro's music?"

"Who doesn't?" she demanded. She hummed a few bars.

Kanno-san chuckled and said, "You're singing my song."

"Tadao's theme is the most beautiful melody in anime," Kiyoko replied.

"It's incredible that you showed up here," Alexa told Matsumoto-san. "One of Kiyoko's dreams was to meet you."

"Ah, so," Matsumoto-san said as Kiyoko nodded excitedly.

"I'm in the Entertainment division at the magazine,"

❝New York is not Tokyo. Not safe.❞

she said. She couldn't remember if she had already said that. Her mind was blanking out. "So if I could interview you both, it would be such an honor."

"We're in town for a few days," Matsumoto-san told her. "You could come to the office."

"Oh, I would totally love to!" Kiyoko cried in English.

He reached into his pant pocket and pulled out a leather business-card case. In the Japanese style, he reached into the case, extracted a card, put the case back into his pocket, and presented it to Kiyoko with both hands. She took it, her heart pumping. *Matsumoto Studios, 664 Fifth Avenue, New York.*

"We don't have *meishi*," she said, using the Japanese word for business card. "I'm so sorry."

"You're students," he said, by way of excusing her. "It's all right. Call my secretary tomorrow and we'll set up a time. We're only in town until Friday."

Fantastic! Today was only Monday.

"Thank you. Thank you so much!" she said.

"We should go," Alexa murmured. "It's almost twelve thirty."

"Two young girls out so late," Matsumoto-san said. "New York is not Tokyo. Not safe."

"We're cabbing it," Kiyoko assured him. She turned and waved her hand, and a cab glided to the curb. "See? No worries."

She bowed deeply. Alexa did the same. Then they hopped in and sped away.

"I can't believe I just met Shinichiro Matsumoto and Jiro Kanno," Kiyoko breathed. "What an amazing night. It was fate that my wallet got stolen. If I hadn't gone back there, I would never have met my idols."

"You have a guardian angel," Alexa agreed. "Or not," she murmured as they came within sight of their building. "Look."

Ay, caramba, there were more lights on in the Lyrics' apartment *and* a light on in the kitchen. Plus a shadow moving across the frosted glass.

Both girls stared at the shadow. Then Kiyoko said to the cabbie, "Let us off at the other end of the block, James."

He didn't answer—maybe because the name on his cab medallion was not James but Sayid—but he did as she requested. Kiyoko pulled out more bills and gave them to him, saying, "Keep the change."

He didn't even grunt, just peeled off with a squeal of his tires. Kiyoko winced, but, really, no one was going to pay any special attention to traffic noise.

Like the commandos they were, the two darted into the alley—yes, a dark alley in SoHo at twelve thirty at night—and hightailed it back into the Dumpster quadrant.

The eau de parfum of steamed garbage rose from the closed lid of the one nearest Kiyoko.

"I'll help you up to the bottom of the fire escape," Kiyoko told Alexa, lacing her fingers together and bending forward to give Alexa a leg up onto the suspended fire escape.

Alexa hoisted herself up and crawled along the section. Then she hit the actual stairs and waved to Kiyoko. Kiyoko herself was taller than Alexa, so she was able to grab on and do a pull-up; then she swung her legs over and onto the steps. She briefly considered a career as a Shaolin warrior monk, discarded the idea—*bad outfits, worse pay*—and together they stealthily made their way up the entire twelve flights of the fire escape; they were sweating and puffing by the time Kiyoko unlocked the back door and silently pushed it open.

Erk. Now there was a light on in the loft itself.

Her eyes huge, Kiyoko backed up, urging Alexa outside. She pulled the door but didn't close it all the way. Instead, she put her ear against the door and listened.

Footsteps padded on the cement floor. Running water, probably in the kitchen. A clank, like silverware on a plate. Midnight snack.

Kiyoko drummed her fingers against the knuckles of her left hand, which was clutching her purse.

"I have to pee," Alexa whispered.

Kiyoko made the universal gesture for silence.

They looked at each other, Alexa perhaps having the

> **She briefly considered a career as a Shaolin warrior monk, discarded the idea–bad outfits, worse pay . . .**

same thought as Kiyoko: *It's Emma, and she's waiting for us.* All at once, the fun left. What if tonight's caper got them booted? Kiyoko's parents would be furious. Grandmama would clutch her heart and moan. To add insult to mortal wounds, Kiyoko would probably have to spend the rest of the summer on Hokkaido. No need to worry about a curfew there: There was nowhere to go.

At long, long, *long* last, the light in the loft went out. With a long, grateful sigh, Alexa urged Kiyoko to open the door. They were quick and silent as ninjas as they hurried through the Flirt-cave, then into the downstairs bathroom, where Alexa gratefully did her thing.

Then, as they wound up the spiral staircase and Kiyoko cracked open the door to their bedroom, the light above the entryway blazed on.

Startled out of her wits, Kiyoko whirled around, bashing into Alexa, who knocked softly against the wall with a sharp little, *"Ay!"*

"Where have you two been?" Mel demanded. "I've been worried sick!"

In answer, Kiyoko held up her wallet and led the way into their room.

"Oh my God!" Mel cried, then dropped her voice to

a whisper. "Where did you find it?"

"It was quite an adventure," Alexa said.

"Too right," Kiyoko agreed.

Kiyoko plopped down on her bed, and told Mel the Vlad Moscow portion of the story.

When she was finished, Mel covered her mouth with both her hands, while Alexa buried her face in her pillow to stifle hysterical laughter.

"What is wrong with you, you lunatic?" Kiyoko demanded. "You were there! It was not in the least amusing!"

"It's just . . . so bad it's funny," Alexa said, wiping her eyes. "You thought you were interviewing this musician, and it's an *idiota* who works in a gelato store, and he steals your wallet!"

"That *is* so bad, it's funny," Mel said. "It would make a good story."

"One you'll take to your grave, mate," Kiyoko said. "Or at least until I'm thirty. Do you want them to send me packing?"

"Okay, this caper is off the record," Mel promised as she sat on her bed. "So why was he in the theater?"

"Because it's a good movie!" Kiyoko said, and then she burst into laughter, too.

"Shut up!" Alexa managed, stifling herself. She was wiping her eyes. "We are going to be so busted!"

"You're spot-on," Kiyoko said. She tossed her wallet into the air and caught it. "If Emma ever found out—"

There was a creak.

Of a floorboard.

In the hall.

The three girls stopped talking and held their breath. Alexa's eyes were practically spinning. Mel looked freaked but far more composed. Of course, *she* had done nothing wrong.

Putting her finger to her lips, Kiyoko continued talking as she carefully unfolded her legs and got off Alexa's bed.

"So it was a lucky thing that I found my wallet in the pocket of my raincoat," she said, crossing the room.

"Very lucky," Mel answered. "Good karma."

"*Gracias a Dios,*" Alexa added emotionally, actually crossing herself.

Kiyoko put her hand around their doorknob, twisted it, and gave the door a soundless push.

There was no one there.

She tiptoed back on down into the main room, which appeared to be empty. The lights were off. All she heard was the whirr of the air conditioning.

There are only two people I really, really hope did not spy on us, she thought to herself. *And one of them would be calling me back into her apartment right now so she could really let me have it, if she had been the one.*

Which leaves Gen. Maybe Mel woke her up by accident. They shared the same bedroom.

"Kiyoko?" someone whispered behind her.

She jerked as if she'd been shot, and whirled around. It was Liv, in a monogrammed white silk bathrobe, carrying a cup of tea.

"Oh," Kiyoko said. "Having trouble sleeping?"

"It's all right, I'm not going to say a word," Liv said softly. "Although I *must* know if you two wore your pajamas on this adventure."

Kiyoko pretended to be insulted. "Excuse me, lad, but today's fashion-forward person can wear pajamas anytime she wants."

"Indeed." Liv smiled and shook her head. "You two."

"We two," Kiyoko concurred.

"Those are your idols," Liv said. "Those two men you ran into?"

Kiyoko nodded. "I'm going to interview them. Trey has *got* to persuade Bishop to let that be my piece. It would be such a . . . a thing for me."

"It does sound spot-on," Liv agreed. "Well, you can talk to him about it tomorrow."

⊙　　⊙　　⊙　　⊙

So she did. She went straight to his office after he rolled in at ten thirty and said, "Mr. Narkisian, sir, I had the most amazing encounter last night! I met Jiro Kanno and Shinichiro Matsumoto, and they said I could interview them for the magazine!"

He looked unimpressed. "I'm drawing a blank."

"The gods of anime! I saw them at *Rustle*." That was almost a lie, but the literal truth could get her busted. "I asked them for an exclusive interview for *Flirt*." She beamed at him proudly. "That would be such a score!"

The right side of Trey's face quirked up in a smile that called to mind the happier Trey of days past as he said, "For them, or for us?"

"Oh. Us, us," she assured him.

He said, "Hmm, let me think about it," and got back to whatever was more important.

She tromped back to her desk. He had sent an article Caitlain had written about product placement in video games to read with a notation, *"Help her with screen grabs."*

Cool, cool, cool! She could *so* do that. Hiro played all those blasted games, and she had to admit that she and Matteo both had wasted many hours using his Xbox when he wasn't home.

Then some mail arrived in her in-box. She clicked it open and read: *Katja Melencourts Jewelry Trunk Sale Tonight:* Flirt *Employees 20% Discount.*

There were some pix of truly luscious chandeliery earrings and dangly pendants. The prices were well within the budgetary constraints of a Katsuda—because there weren't all that many, ha—and Kiyoko hunkered down, admiring the work. She made jewelry, too, though she tended to rip apart action figures and use their body parts to make oversize pins and things. At the thought, her fingers itched to make some art.

"Book call!" That was Liss, who was staggering up the corridor behind a stack of novels and coffee-table books. They were the books their various reviewers—both on-staff and freelance—had no interest in. The Entertainment people divided them up.

"Ooh, ooh!" Kiyoko cried, hopping from her desk to meet Liss in the aisle. She grabbed part of the literary tower and said, "What's good?"

"I call dibs on the Warhol book," Liss said. She grinned at Kiyoko. "Obviously."

"You're a sucker for an unhappy ending," Kiyoko shot back.

They both laughed. Liss tilted her head and said, "I'm gonna miss you." A beat. "I'm going to be leaving about the same time as you."

Kiyoko's smile faded. "Oh, no. Oh, I am so sorry. When you said . . ."

"I'm not getting fired. I'm quitting," Liss explained. "I just gave my almost-two-weeks' notice."

"Then I didn't guess in a million years," Kiyoko said.

Liss smiled. "After we interviewed Geff Wilcox, I called him. We got together, and I showed him some songs I wrote. He wants to buy them, and his manager offered me a position in his agency, managing some of his smaller clients. So I'm quitting and moving to Los Angeles."

Kiyoko gaped at her. "Just like that?"

Liss shrugged. "Yeah."

"But you . . . you said you didn't have the stuff."

Liss swiveled right and left with her pile of books in her arms. "The stuff for this gig. This isn't me." She rolled her eyes. "I am so glad I found that out so fast."

"But . . . how did you find out?" Kiyoko asked. "How did you know?"

Liss gave her a long, understanding look and said, "Let me buy you lunch."

They went to a nearby deli. Kiyoko got the Devourer, which was her favorite: turkey, ham, salami, *and* meatballs. The mere sight of it usually sent Mel into a tizzy.

> ## " You're a sucker for an unhappy ending. "

Before she forgot, Kiyoko gave Liss back her tape recorder. She was amazed by the difference in Liss. Where yesterday she was a nervous wreck, today she was all confidence. As she stabbed at her pasta salad and gobbled it down, Liss said, "How are things going for you at *Flirt*?"

Kiyoko started to give her what her little brother called "TV talk"—the usual malarkey one handed out during superficial social encounters. But Kiyoko sensed this wasn't a superficial encounter. Liss really wanted to know.

"Things with me and Trey are a little not so fantastic," she admitted.

"Something's going on," Liss said, chewing and nodding, nodding and chewing. "I would think he would give you some hints about what it is, at least. You're his intern."

"It's like he's not listening to me," Kiyoko said. "I have the chance to interview these total gods of anime, and he's like, 'Uh-huh, whatever.' They're only in town until Friday. I don't know what to do."

"Call them and schedule it," Liss advised. She picked up her juicy hamburger and took a big bite. "Don't wait for Trey to give you permission. Look what happened with me and Geff." She dabbed some ketchup off the corner of her mouth with her red-and-white checked paper napkin. "Make your own luck, Kiyoko."

Kiyoko sat up straight and squared her shoulders. "I can do that," she said, bobbing her head. "Maybe I can do what you did! I know about their music; I know what they like. Maybe I could compose a few cues to play for them." She raised her brows. "Do you think?"

"Maybe," Liss said. "Is music your thing?"

Kiyoko pondered. "I have a lot of things. I'm kind

'Make your own luck, Kiyoko.'
Kiyoko sat up straight and squared
her shoulders. 'I can do that,'
she said, bobbing her head.

of all over the place," she admitted. "I love movies, books, fashion; I make jewelry . . . of course I'm into music and video games. And I love manga. I don't want to have to choose."

"You're sixteen," Liss said. "Some day you'll have to figure out what exactly you want to do, but you have time."

Kiyoko plucked a meatball out of her sandwich and nibbled on it. The sauce was what made them so good.

"I don't feel like I have time. I feel like I'll be old before I've done half the things I want to do," Kiyoko told her.

"Then may I suggest you stay young as long as possible?" Liss said with a chuckle.

Words to live by, Kiyoko thought.

chapter five

Liss and Kiyoko walked back to the *Flirt* offices from the deli. Kiyoko stopped to admire several store windows, prompting Liss to remind her that she, for one, had to get back to the office.

"They're still paying for my time, y'know," Liss said.

"Well, they're not paying for mine," Kiyoko retorted.

"Thousands of girls would pay anything to be in your place," Liss nudged.

"You're right," Kiyoko agreed.

Liss had a meeting, so she gave Kiyoko a wave and tootled off to that. Kiyoko returned to the Entertainment division with a spring in her step. Music! She was going to make some!

The joint was jumping, folks scurrying hither and thither. Thrash had been replaced with disco, and hideous though it was, Kiyoko found herself wiggling her hips to the beat. Shawn, who had a stack of large manila envelopes in his arms, grabbed one and pretended to fan himself with it.

No sooner had Kiyoko returned to her cubicle, singing "Night Fever" in a high falsetto, than Trey buzzed her.

> ## "This is a test, Kiyoko."

"Sim?" she said, meaning "yes" in Portuguese.

"Water tank," was all he said. And all he needed to say.

"Consuelo," she replied with a groan. "Trey . . ."

The sigh. The bloody sigh.

She hung her head. "I'm sorry."

"You can make it up to me. I still have three months' worth of Spotteds that need to be proofed, and no one's free."

Except me. Ha ha. "I'm happy to do that," she pleaded.

"I need them tomorrow for a planning meeting."

"They'll be ready," she swore by whatever political deity spun her karmic wheel.

"This is a test, Kiyoko."

"I know, Trey. I *so* know." She clenched her fist. "And I will not fail you."

He did not sigh. But he did grunt. He said, "E-mail Jer and tell him to send you the file."

"On it," she assured him. She immediately looked Jer up in the online directory to get his addy, and dashed off the request.

Then she sat back, chock-full of protein and

ambition. Liss knew how to mix it up. She'd make some musical cues to show Matsumoto and Kanno. Wouldn't it be amazing if they actually bought them, like Geff Wilcox had bought Liss's stuff?

Reaching into her hood-purse, Kiyoko located the sacred business card for Matsumoto Studios. She punched in the number with a *woot-woot* and got the receptionist, who had a Japanese accent.

Kiyoko spoke to her in Japanese, explaining who she was. The receptionist—Hayeda-san—had been briefed, and she suggested to Katsuda-san that Friday at four would be a good time. Hmm. Matsumoto and Kanno were heading back to Tokyo that night. And Kiyoko's workday at *Flirt* was officially over at five. So that meant that if Trey wasn't interested, she'd have to figure out a way to get there under her own steam.

Not a problem for Kiyoko Katsuda, plucky girl intern. Everything was falling into place. Nicely.

She opened her wallet and grinned at her fortune-cookie fortune. Then she pulled out her Razr and texted Matteo.

KIYoKO!!!: M? Doko ni?
MATTeO: KikO! Tomorrow leaving
   Tokyo 4 Calif.
KIYoKO!!!: Wah! Will miss being
   together 4 Ur bday!
MATTeO: Miss U now!

XXXXOXOXOX
KIYoKO!!!: Guess what!
   Going to compose musik 4
   Kanno & Matsumoto!
MATTeO: Kewl. They R?

Kiyoko's flying fingers paused. Matteo wasn't into anime the way she was, but surely he remembered the names of her idols. She talked about them all the time.

When I'm not talking about bands or movies or cool stuff to download, she reminded herself. *It may be difficult for the lad to keep up.*

KIYoKO!!!: Anime! Geniuses!
MATTeO: Banzai!

"That's the spirit," Kiyoko said. Her *tomo-boyu* might be ignorant on some counts, but he was certainly supportive.

She e-mailed Jer about the Spotteds again. Then the dreaded Hilda, who was maybe sixty but did tai chi and yoga and looked like a Viking goddess, appeared in her cubicle with eleven or twelve kilos of folders in her arms and said, "Filing time."

Bleh.

      ◉   ◉   ◉   ◉

It was nearly five by the time Jer e-mailed with

the darn Spotteds. Kiyoko realized that she was going to have to take them home, so she forwarded the file to her personal account and took off, finding her mates. Off to Nobu before she settled in to do right by her liege. They ordered shrimp tempura, handrolls, and sushi. As usual, Mel and Alexa got quiet because it was expensive, and she and Liv had to explain to them that it would be no fun to chow down while the two of them sat there insisting that all they wanted was miso soup.

"Wish they'd bring us sake," Kiyoko grumbled.

But of course they would not, and they toasted Alexa's snap of Brad Pitt with green tea.

"And to my new career as a composer!" Kiyoko cried, raising her teacup. "I'm going to write some cues to take to Matsumoto and Kanno."

Liv cocked a brow. "I didn't know you were a musician."

Alexa nodded vigorously. "Oh, *sí*, she has some nice music programs. She's state-of-the-art."

Kiyoko smiled at her. Loyal Alexa. So sweet. Also, a bit prone to exaggeration.

"I've a few things," Kiyoko said modestly.

"Up your sleeve," Alexa said, and they both laughed.

Mel chimed in. "Be sure to ask us for help if there's anything we can do."

Kiyoko bowed. "*Arigato gozaimashita.*" Which, in Japan, meant thank you very much.

They got back to the loft at about sevenish. Emma looked like she was about to faint. Gen and Charlotte were out, which added to the good karma.

Kiyoko trotted into her bedroom while the others stayed in the main room to watch the telly for a bit. Humming, Kiyoko flipped open her laptop and downloaded the file from Jer.

SPOTTED! Mary-Kate or was it Ashley? Unknown very hot man in tow, carrying three Prada bags.

Kiyoko scrolled down. And down. And down.

She looked at the bottom of the document to see the page counter. Then she did a word count.

A hundred pages? Fifty thousand words?

Panic washed over her in waves. For a moment she couldn't even think of the English words she needed.

She staggered back into the living room. Liv saw her first, and half-rose from the deep red couch.

"Kiyoko?"

"Lads, I need your help."

Her brain came back online, and she explained the situation.

"Oh, my God," Mel breathed. "That's a lot to dump on someone who isn't used to copyediting. Did you know it was that much?"

Kiyoko's heart was trying very hard to leap from her chest. "No. He did say three months, but . . . in three months there are twelve book reviews, do you know what I'm saying? She felt dizzy. "Lads, I can*not* fail. Trey will exile my butt outta here." She cast her eyes down. "Or even worse, force me to file for Hilda for the next two weeks."

"Okay, this is my area," Mel announced. "Kiyoko, download everything to your computer, then batch it up and e-mail it to each of us. That's only twenty-five pages for each of us. If we all pitch in . . ." She looked meaningfully at Liv and Alexa.

"I'm in," Liv assured her.

"Yo también," Alexa said.

"Oh, God, thank you," Kiyoko said in a grateful rush.

Moving fast, Kiyoko batched the Spotteds into smaller files and sent three of them to Melanie, Alexa, and Liv. Her friends fwapped open their laptops in unison like commandos.

Then she said, "I'll go brew a pot of coffee." She picked up her own laptop to take with her into the kitchen. She didn't want to waste a single precious second. She rummaged in the freezer for her stash of Blue Mountain roast. When her hand closed around the package, she knew she was in trouble: There wasn't enough for a cup of coffee, much less the pot she had been planning to brew.

I meant to buy more.

She found someone else's coffee and checked the name on the label. Gack! It was Gen's. She put it back. More rummaging revealed Alexa's care package from home, a special blend her mother had sent her. Alexa nearly wept with homesickness every time she drank it.

Kiyoko ground the beans and poured them into the French coffee extractor thingie. Carrying the carafe and four cups back into her room, she found Alexa bent over her computer, reading off a line to Mel, who was looking up from her own laptop with a very concerned look on her face. Kiyoko's last little piece of serenity evaporated.

"Sp&crew8s `!!>. That's what it says," Alexa informed Mel. She looked sideways at Kiyoko as she hovered in the doorway with the coffee.

"I think something is wrong big time," Alexa announced.

Mel said, "Hold on. Let me open mine." Her fingers clattered over the keys.

The next three seconds could have been a year as Kiyoko hurried to Mel's desk and peered over her shoulder.

There was nothing on Mel's screen but garbage.

What if it was the same on her computer, too? A desperate thought flashed through her mind: *Then I'll have the perfect excuse not to have done them.*

Except that I have Trey's cell phone number, and he would have expected me to call him and let him know . . .

She swallowed hard, set down the coffee, and flipped open the lid of her own laptop. She clicked on the file and squinted at the screen, terrified to look.

SPOTTED! Kanye West, on the steps of the Met,

carrying a single red rose.

"We have liftoff!" Kiyoko cried, then stifled herself.

"Good. Then try resending to us," Mel urged her.

But the second attempt resulted in garbage again.

"What's wrong?" Kiyoko wailed.

"Don't panic," Liv counseled her. "There's a way out of this."

"Sure," Mel said. "She can print some out for each of us and we can copyedit them by hand. Then one of us can type in the corrections." She thought a minute. "There's a flaw in that logic. If we can only read the files on her computer . . ." She took a breath. "We'll have to type everything back in and burn whatever each of us does onto a disk. Then she can upload them onto her laptop or her desktop at work."

"But something's wrong if you can't read the files on your computers," Kiyoko said. "The file's been corrupted."

"That may be, but you can read it. Copy it so you have an original you can show him if this doesn't work. As for the part we're doing, typing everything back in is the best solution," Liv said. She gathered up her hair and let it fall as she squared her shoulders. "Well, let's get to it, ladies."

They got to work. By midnight, Kiyoko had finished correcting eight thousand words online and Mel and Alexa each had finished hand-correcting nearly the same amount. Mel had typed back in all of her text, while Alexa was closing in.

But they were drooping. A discreet glance at their work revealed that they were making mistakes. And to be honest, Kiyoko wasn't doing much better.

There. Another done. Yawning, she moved to the next Spotted.

Demi and Ashton strolling down Fifth Avenue.

The IM screen on her laptop flashed:

MATTeO: KikO?
KIYoKO!!!: M? Doko ni?
MATTeO: Airport! U doing what?
  Can't sleep?
KIYoKO!!!: As if! Work!
MATTeO: Grl, it's 1:30 AM there!
KIYoKO!!!: I no! Gottago!
MATTeO: KK! Don't work 2 hard!
  xoxoxoxoxoxox

She sighed.

Alexa began snoring. Mel's head was bobbing. Cross-legged on Kiyoko's bed, Liv sucked in her breath and said to Kiyoko, "I just need a second."

"No," Kiyoko said. "You need to rest. You're going to have your own long day filled with irritating busy work. I don't want you to get in trouble because of me."

"No. I'm fine," Liv insisted.

Kiyoko just waited her out while she proofed another Spotted. Lindsay Lohan, shoe-shopping.

> **_If she had anything on us, she would have said something by now._**

Within five minutes, Liv was asleep.

Ashton and Demi.

Kiyoko squinted. "Demi" looked wrong. But it *was* Demi, right?

Ashton and Demie.

No.

I'm too tired.

Dawn found her working alone, pretty much in despair. She got up and swayed into the kitchen. Maybe there was a power bar somewhere . . .

Then Gen sailed in.

"Good morning." She gave Kiyoko the once-over. "Wow, did you sneak out or something? Have you even been to bed?"

"I never sneak out," Kiyoko insisted.

Gen gave her a look.

Kiyoko slowly turned on two rubbery legs and made her way out of the kitchen.

The alarm in her and Alexa's bedroom was playing salsa, but nobody was stirring. Kiyoko said urgently, "Lads, lads! Wake up!"

Mel sat up first, then Liv, then Alexa; as they put on their bathrobes, she told them what had happened. They had all fallen asleep, and her work wasn't done.

"And Gen is in the kitchen with a smirk and talking about me sneaking out," she finished.

"That doesn't mean anything. Gen is always smirking," Alexa said. "If she had anything on us, she would have said something by now. *Siento*, Kiyoko. I'm sorry we dozed off," she added, trying to hide a huge yawn.

"It's all right. You have to get ready for work," Kiyoko told her, gathering up the printouts with their corrections. She was near tears. "Hey, we did a good job, lads," she said. "It'll be all right." She smiled at them.

They smiled back.

Sort of.

⊙　　⊙　　⊙　　⊙

Kiyoko thought about calling in sick. But it was just too irresponsible. So she decided she had to go in. She got dressed for efficiency in her short plaid skirt, black stockings, combat boots, a black tee, and her little glasses. Then she wound her hair into two ponytails and slipped on the big sports watch she was going to give Matteo for his birthday. He was a Virgo; it was coming up.

Trey didn't usually roll into *Flirt* until around ten. None of the more senior people did. Kiyoko was expected to be there at nine sharp to answer the phone and get Trey's schedule updated, based on calls and e-mails that had come in during the night.

She stuffed her laptop and the printed pages into

the well-worn leather satchel her father had used during his university days, grabbed her third PowerBar, and appeared front and center at the revolving doors to Hudson-Bennett Magazines just as the security guard was unlocking them.

"You're here bright and early," he said by way of greeting, and she flashed him a smile as she sailed up the lift, flashed past the main reception area, and bobbed along the silver-and-glass walls, past rows of empty cubicles.

To *her* desk, where she quickly uploaded the finished Spotteds to her desktop—those on her laptop, and the three disks her friends had used—and began to work on the others.

The others . . . which did not have as many errors as the ones she had already done. She quickly scanned the pages Alexa and Mel had corrected, remembering the missed errors she had noticed. There were fewer than she expected.

Then Liss showed, and asked her what she was doing. Liss summoned Jer, and both of them pitched in.

I am seeing some sunshine!

Kiyoko set to work, too.

The phone rang. She let the voice-mail system grab it as her fingers clattered along, making correction after correction with a steady pace. She glanced at the clock on her screen. Nine twenty.

She kept going.

Nine forty.

Ten sharp.

Her cell phone rang.

She jumped and yanked it out of her bag. Caller ID warned her that it was Trey.

"Good morning," she said cheerily.

"The voice-mail's still on," he replied.

"Blast! On it!" Shutting her eyes tightly, she turned off the system. At once, all three lines started ringing.

"I'll be in late," Trey said tersely.

"Oh, my God, that is *great*!" she shouted. Then she caught herself. "I mean, okay, I'll make a note of that. Do you want me to rearrange your schedule all to hell or cancel things or what?"

"There's a working lunch at one. You'll be going."

"Got it." She paused. "Those Spotteds. Certainly were a lot of them."

"What are you talking about?"

"The text you wanted me to go through? The fifty thousand words?"

"What?"

"Yes," she said, nodding.

"That's ridiculous. That must be for the entire year. There should have been fif*teen* thousand words or so."

"Oh, my God," she muttered.

"You did all that? Well, this is . . . nice. Okay, listen, when I get in, we're going to have a talk."

"Oh, my God," she muttered again. Then she said brightly, "You know where to find me."

He hung up.

Liss and Jer had other tasks to attend to. At eleven forty-one, reeling with exhaustion, Kiyoko put the finishing touches on the last Spotted. She'd been sweating bullets; the stupid phone wouldn't stop ringing. It seemed that everyone needed something from Entertainment: permissions, fact-checks, the phone number of someone's publicist. She was Ms. Assertiveness as she wrote down all the requests, saying, "I'm sorry, I'm doing something for Trey right now, but I'll get to your thingamabob as soon as I can."

Her mates snuck in to see her.

"We were going to spend our lunch hours helping you, but turns out we're all going to that lunch thing." Mel sat at Kiyoko's desktop, resplendent in hippie chic—a flowery lavender skirt and a crocheted tank dressed up with lace. She scrolled through the entries, moving her lips as she read them.

> **There's a working lunch at one. You'll be going.**

"*Sí*, we're going to the lunch," Alexa informed her, moving to Kiyoko's chair as Mel rose and gestured for her to take a spin. She had on olive capris and a purple-and-olive tank. She had wound her hair into a messy bun and slid a *Flirt* pen through it.

"It's all anyone is talking about." Liv was picture-perfect in walking shorts and a slouchy jacket from Dries

Van Noten. "They're rather upset about it, actually."

Kiyoko wished she had the energy to care.

KIYOKO'S BLOG:

Does no good deed go unpunished? It seems that the harder I try to do a good job, the worse it is. I was doing better when I shot from the hip. I wrote my application for this internship two hours before the cutoff. Faxed it to the wrong place, resent it . . . and got in. Maybe there is a lesson there . . .

MOOD: A BIT TICKED, ACTUALLY

MUSIC: "Run It" by Chris Brown

The phone rang. Kiyoko grabbed it up, trilling, "Muzak department."

"Is Alexa there?" It was Lynn, and she sounded angry enough to chew through wood.

Kiyoko's scratchy eyes widened as she gazed at the girl in question. "Alexa?" she echoed.

Alexa paled and wildly shook her head. She, Liv, and Mel scooted away from Kiyoko's desk and hurried down the glass-and-silver corridor.

"No," Kiyoko said. "Bloody sorry."

"I need her *now*." *Grrrroaou!*

"Well, ah, I'm sure she's around," Kiyoko said. "And working very hard, might I add. She's always talking in the

> **Her pride turned to acute anxiety as he stopped, scrolled back up, reread something, then nodded and moved on.**

loft about how hard she works. Not that she complains. Because she loves it. Working hard. Puritan ethic. No wonder they all left merry old England."

"If you see her, tell her I am—Alexa! Where *have* you been?"

The phone disconnected.

Just then, Trey burst through the doors and looked at her expectantly.

"Thank you for calling," Kiyoko concluded, hanging up the phone. She looked up at Trey and said, "That was nothing."

"Okay, let me see what this is all about." He held out his hand.

"See," she said as she put a CD into his palm. She followed him down the hall and into his office. He sat down at his desk and inserted the disk into his desktop, settling in as the file opened. He began to read. Her pride turned to acute anxiety as he stopped, scrolled back up, reread something, then nodded and moved on. Reggae music poured down the hall, and someone was singing along in falsetto. The music of the good old happy days. Sweet.

As he scrolled onward, ever onward, he said, "What else do I have to do?"

"There's a list," she said. There was always a list. Much of her day was spent compiling lists.

He said nothing, and she realized he was waiting for her to go get it.

She tottered back down to her cubicle and retrieved the list, such as it was. Then she returned to Trey's office. He was on the phone, and he was actually smiling; it was so unexpected that she let out a little whoop, which he either didn't hear or ignored. He said into the phone, "Yes, it's a done deal."

She wondered if he was talking about the possibility that he might be fired. But if that were the case, why the joy?

Then he hung up and said, "This will be interesting, Kiyoko. You're about to watch a

> **" This will be interesting, Kiyoko. You're about to watch a coup. "**

coup." He tipped his head and gazed up at her with his Mr. Serious face. "You have less than two weeks left. Things are about to get radically different. Still want to be my intern?"

"Hell, yeah," she blurted.

He laughed. She hadn't heard him laugh in a month of Sundays. He said, "Okay. Here's the deal. Bishop was about to can me. But I figured out a way to make myself very valuable. I worked hard, and I studied all the angles, and I went way out on a limb. And it's going to pay off."

He checked his watch. "Now. It's showtime, Kiyoko. You ready?"

"Roger that," she said boldly.

With another laugh, he rose from his desk and slid a beautiful light gray silk jacket off a wooden hanger suspended from his coat rack. It was very ooh-lala.

Just one problem: Before they went off to savor savory chicken tikka masala, basmati rice, and puffy hot naan, Kiyoko wanted Trey to tell her that she had done a fabulous job on the Spotteds and that he was very proud of her. She was like his little dachshund, looking for her treat. But he said nothing.

They began to walk. People were leaving their cubicles, apparently to go to the lunch, too. The poster-size eyes of Jake Gyllenhaal, taped to a door, followed her as she loped along beside Trey. Everyone was edgy.

Kiyoko said, "Are heads going to roll?"

"You betcha," Trey replied.

chapter six

Trey and Kiyoko cabbed it to a very cool-looking Indian restaurant called Rani. The place smelled all spicy, like a Buddhist temple. Trey looked all fancy, like a department head at *Flirt*.

Kiyoko wanted to know what was going on. "Come on. I'm your *intern*. The suspense will knock me dead—"

All-mystery guy, he put his finger to his lips.

The private dining room was decorated in gilt and sparkling pictures of Ganesha and Krishna. There was a waterfall and a lot of dark, ornate wood. Kiyoko's weary feet sank into soft green carpet; a kilometer or two away, a veeerrry long table was set for the entire borough of Manhattan—or maybe two dozen people.

"Is this where *she* tucks in?" Kiyoko asked him. "Like, with the prime minister?"

"The food will be excellent," Trey promised. The old Trey sparkled in his eyes. He was definitely back in the game, whatever game that was. She was reassured, intrigued, and ready for whatever wacky high jinks were about to ensue. Resolutely she back-burnered her exhaustion and squared her shoulders.

The department heads were there in their warrior gear—i.e., everything that was drop-dead fashion-forward. Versace, Prada, McCartney. It was one of those heady moments where she had to pinch herself in order to be certain that she wasn't dreaming. Kiyoko Katsuda got to do a lot of cool stuff, but this was definitely one of the coolest.

She saw Liv and her boss, Demetria. Alexa and Lynn. Bishop and Mel had apparently not yet arrived. Everyone else was smiling nervously, and no wonder, if they didn't know what was going on, either. It seemed to her that Liss had an excellent sense of timing, getting out before someone did it for her.

Kiyoko inhaled the extremely wonderful spices—curry and coriander—wafting from the double doors at the opposite end of the huge room. Perfumes mingled. Everyone milled around with drink glasses in their hands. All Kiyoko saw to fill them with were bottles of mineral water.

Trey said, "We never drink during these things. Which is good." He tapped his head. "It's important to keep your wits about yourself at confabs."

She pretended to write a list in the air. "Wits. Aye-aye, captain."

Just then, a woman Kiyoko had never met swept over. She was as thin as a whippet and her hair was midnight black against pale skin. She had on a teeny black tent dress and flats.

She said, "Trey. I know the interns are assigned to various department heads, such as yourself. But if you could explain to your intern that she should fulfill simple interdepartmental requests, and I *so* do not need the attitude, all right?" Then she swiveled her head and glared at Kiyoko, who felt like she had been socked in the stomach.

Trey cocked a brow and said, "Sorry?"

"She knows what I'm talking about," the woman shot back and glided away.

"Trey, I don't," Kiyoko protested. "I didn't . . ." She thought a moment and closed her eyes. "I was . . . checking the Spotteds, and I did ask a couple of people to call back later."

"That's no sin," he said. "Were you basically polite?"

"Basically," she said.

She took a breath, about to remind him that she had been forced to do an unreasonable amount of work because of someone else's blunder.

But just at that moment, it was all about Bishop.

Top Diva swept in, swathed in a form-fitting all-white suit and black pearls. Kiyoko was not a suit wearer, but she had to admit the excellent tailoring put the luster on Bishop's megaexecutive look. Bishop's little terrier-woman, Delia, was bustling behind her with a BlackBerry

> ## " She was still wearing her headset, and Kiyoko wondered if she wore it to bed. "

or a PDA or something; she was speaking into a headset just like always. Delia was totally jacked in; and Bishop was always jacking her around. Kiyoko figured that she herself would last a day working that closely with the imperious woman.

"Everyone," Ms. Bishop said, giving her hands a little clap. "Find your seats."

Each place was set with a white charger, then a white luncheon plate atop of which sat a white napkin folded origami-style like maybe a crane. The plates were guarded by five thousand knives, forks, and spoons. Kiyoko was not worried. She could hold her own at a formal meal. She hoped Mel would be okay.

There were also name cards, each white card inserted into a polished brass oval. Kiyoko had a moment when she wondered if the *Flirt* interns would be segregated from the people who held actual paying jobs. But after wandering a few chairs to her left, she located a *Flirt* holder that said *Kiyoko Katsuda*. She would be seated to Trey's left.

On Kiyoko's left was Gen Bishop, and then Gen's boss, Naomi. Oh, yay.

And here was the little rascal now, gorgeous in a highly appropriate Sue Wong embroidered dress. A flicker of "oh must you exist?" crossed Gen's features before she smiled her cloying, overly sweet smile and shifted one-sixteenth of an inch to the left, as if she were giving ground to Kiyoko so she could pull out her chair. Or trying to avoid her like the plague.

Liv was seated three chairs down and across the table, between Demetria, her boss, and Quinn, the managing editor.

Bishop sat at the head of the table. Delia sat directly next to Bishop, like a medieval food taster or something. She was still talking into her headset, and Kiyoko wondered if she wore it to bed. Mel was on Bishop's left, and Kiyoko watched her watching Bishop for etiquette pointers. Kiyoko reminded herself to tell Mel that she would need to know this stuff for when she won the Nobel Prize for literature and had to eat with the king of Sweden.

The players continued to take their places. Alexa and Lynn sat next to Charlotte and *her* boss, a marathoner type who was smiling up at a waiter as he unfurled her napkin crane and laid it across her lap. He reminded Kiyoko of a bullfighter. *Olé!*

The heavenly scents from the kitchen kicked up a notch. Trey had briefed her in the cab. First they would eat. The purpose of the monthly lunches was usually to bring them all onto the same page. Each department had studies and proposals and CD-ROMs on Ms. Bishop's desk all the time, and there had to be a way to disseminate the information.

"But today it's a whole new game," he informed

> **Without warning, a wave of dizziness rushed through Kiyoko, and she clenched her hood-purse between her fists.**

her. "Watch. Learn." He smiled at her, and she was a butterfly, transformed from a thickheaded dolt who couldn't find a piece of paper to write down a phone number to a fellow shrewd fashion-magazine politico.

She looked up and down the table and realized that everyone else had fallen silent. They were giving Bishop their full attention. Without warning, a wave of dizziness rushed through Kiyoko, and she clenched her hood-purse between her fists.

A waiter approached, unfolding her crane napkin and draping it over her lap. Her guy was not a bullfighter; he was more of the dentist variety.

"All right, let's begin," Bishop announced.

It was as if someone had banged a gong: Waiters with huge stainless-steel trays loaded with platters started pouring out of the double doors. Kiyoko nodded with delight as each waiter in turn asked if he might place a tiny morsel on her plate. Soon it was dotted with brilliant dollops of her favorite dishes on the planet.

Once Bishop took the first bite, Kiyoko picked up her fork and started eating. Beside her, Trey was kind of goosey, not so much eating as pretending to eat.

"Naan?" a waiter asked Kiyoko, flourishing a plate brimming with flat, doughy disks of bread.

"Sure." She let him drape it on her bread plate with a pair of stainless-steel tongs before she picked it back up, the whole piece, and ripped off a section with gusto. As she lustily chewed, she felt eyes on her and glanced in Liv's direction. She had a piece of naan, too, and was flaking it into minuscule, feathery wisps that she then palmed into her mouth, as if it would be entirely too gauche to actually be caught eating the stuff. After all, it was against the law in England to take a photograph of Queen Elizabeth with her mouth full.

Trey started talking to the person to his right, leaving Kiyoko to contemplate the possibility of speaking to Gen.

Nah.

Then Gen said, "You guys were sneaking around all night last night."

"Sneaking implies . . . stealth," Kiyoko said. "It's not possible to sneak around in my own home."

"The loft is not your home," Gen retorted. "Two more weeks and you'll never see it again."

"Unlike you," Kiyoko said. "This is what, your fifth summer doing this? You ever consider you are in a rut?"

Gen sighed. "I don't know why I bother."

"I was working," Kiyoko informed her.

"All night?"

"I'm like that. Have some naan," Kiyoko said devilishly, offering her the rest of her slab.

KIYOKO'S BLOG:

It seems my ability to piss some people off is directly proportional to how conformist they are. Gen, Gen Junior (Charlotte), and Liv—to a far lesser extent—live for using the right fork. Gen wants everyone to do a cover of what's happening now. But I'm with Trey—I'm all about what's gonna happen. I live for the surprise.
MOOD: Intrigued!
MUSIC: SITAR MUZAK! IT ROCKS!

Maybe she was punchy, but her revelation pleased her big-time. She turned to Trey with what felt like a goony look on her face. He smiled at her and said, "Are you feeling all right?"

She nodded.

"Eat," he said, looking Trey—ha ha—amused. He was so kitty-cat pleased with himself. She studied the other department heads. No one else was acting quite as *gleeful* as Trey was.

So she ate. In her lap, her hood-purse vibrated and she knew she had a message or a call. Surreptitiously she drew her phone out a sliver and glanced at the display.

SPIDER_K: ANSR? CLUBBING 2NIGHT?

Hmm, how unwise was it to answer? Delia was yakking on her headset, and Bishop was pushing two whole threads of cucumber onto her fork, so Kiyoko decided to text quickly back.

KIYoKO!!!: NEIN!
SPIDER_K: :(!!!!

She chuckled to herself. Spider was obviously insane. But she couldn't go clubbing. She had to work on her music for Jiro Kanno!

After three years the waiters descended on the table like fire ants and whisked all the plates, silverware, and crumbs away, leaving behind only water glasses and memories. There was rice pudding for dessert, which few of the fit, thin diners allowed anywhere near them. It was accompanied by strong Turkish coffee served in tiny cloisonné thimble cups with lemon twists and raw sugar cubes.

"Dear God, yes," Kiyoko told the waiter when he asked her if she would care for some.

Then the room went silent again; Kiyoko figured there was a secret code: "Bishop is going to talk, pass it on" that she just hadn't learned yet.

Madame commanded their attention; all eyes were on her. As tired as she was, Kiyoko felt energized just looking at her. There was something Bishop had; some kind of aura. Kiyoko was in awe of it. She wanted some of it.

"Our demographic has shifted right out from under us," she said without any warm-up whatsoever. "We are skewing old. This is not news to any of you, but it's a bigger problem than we thought. And it's not your fault."

People moved in their seats, looking anxious. Maybe it was not their fault, but it didn't mean their heads weren't going to roll because of it. It was clear this was not the script they were expecting. They didn't know what was coming next. Maybe layoffs.

"Our readers are plugging in," Bishop continued. "You all know that we're getting more hits on our website every week. We have been assuming that they're going to the website after they read the book. But we're wrong."

The anxious heads nodded, because that was what heads did in situations like these. *Yes! We're wrong! Megawrong! Whatever you say!* Even Kiyoko was nodding like a bobblehead.

Bishop kept going. "Twenty-three percent go to the website first. And twelve percent of those don't ever read *Flirt* in hard copy."

Kiyoko's brows shot up. That *was* a shocker.

"Our readers get their information from so many more sources than they did even a year ago. *Flirt* kept

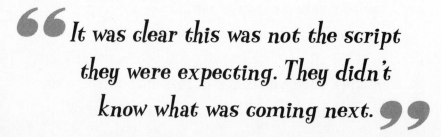

It was clear this was not the script they were expecting. They didn't know what was coming next.

up . . . for a while . . . by referencing those sources in the book. But if they're not reading the book . . ." She waited for everyone to draw their own conclusions. Kiyoko's mind was working overtime, but she wasn't quite there yet with her deductions.

Bishop went on. "Our online presence has been incredible." She smiled at Quinn. "And we need to think of that online presence as our primary publication, not the stepsister of the book. That's why I'm announcing today that we're going after the heavy users of electronic media with a vengeance. We're going to produce content they can access on their cell phones, BlackBerries, Treos, and iPods, and push their ability to interface with us."

The room began to buzz. Kiyoko hazarded a look over her shoulder at Trey, who was staring down at his cell phone and grinning.

She was beyond intrigued. Trey was no moron. If he was taking calls during Top Diva's speech, then he had good reason.

He glanced up at her and gave her a little wink. Then her cell phone vibrated. She jumped. She knew it was Trey.

It's coup time! she realized excitedly.

Stealthily she drew out her phone and stared down at the display.

TNARKISIAN: Here it comes.

". . . *Flirt* remains a venue for haute couture, for the highest and best of art, fashion, beauty, and fitness. Our journalists have received numerous awards and accolades for their fine reporting." There was color in Bishop's cheeks, like her cheekbones were on fire.

"But we need to deliver our world to *participants,* not readers. From now on, we are about interactivity. We will give our consumers multiple opportunities to become part of the editorial process, inviting them to begin their partnership with us through the e-media and then go on to the book. As of today, we are creating a full-service *Flirt* network, and I must say I couldn't be more excited about it."

The table burst into applause, some of it genuine.

Bishop pointed at Kiyoko—*no, at Trey!*—and said, "It was Trey's passionate argument for this redesign that persuaded me to engage some of the savviest media consultants in the world. They echoed Trey's opinions. Therefore, effective in three months, Trey will become co-managing editor in charge of Electronic Content, working directly with Quinn."

Oh my God, talk about a great leap forward! Kiyoko was about to shriek with happiness as more applause rolled around the table. She wondered if there would be champagne now.

Gen looked like she was swallowing ground glass as she said to Kiyoko, "Wow, your boss just got a major bump up."

"Yeah. Big surprise, eh?" she added, looking savvy.

Inwardly, Kiyoko exulted. She was the intern princess, that was for sure.

The applause died down as Bishop continued. "We began a search for a suitable replacement for Trey as head of Entertainment a month ago." The dragon lady surveyed her vassals. "We're very pleased to announce that Belle Holder will be taking that position."

There was more applause as Kiyoko traded stunned looks with Mel, Alexa, and Liv. Belle Holder was a *god* in the music industry. A regular columnist for *Rolling Stone,* someone you saw on every cool channel, who attended every cool party . . .

"We'll be looking for brilliance, Trey," Ms. Bishop threatened him.

"Thank you, Ms. Bishop," he said, composed and relaxed, like he had never worried about a thing in his life and never would.

"A précis describing our reorganization has been e-mailed to each of you," Bishop announced to the table at large. "We'll reconvene as a group at the end of the week, once you've had a chance to study it. Trey will be working closely with Quinn and me as they find their way. I'm sure they'll be in touch."

Across the table, Liv raised her water glass in salute. Alexa gave Kiyoko a "now what?" look and Mel was listening to Bishop, who was saying something directly to her at the opposite end of the table from Kiyoko.

"This lunch is over," Bishop added abruptly as she

pushed away from the table. Beside her, Delia leaped to her feet, leaned down, and picked up a big black briefcase. She was like a mobile desk.

Kiyoko turned to congratulate her newly knighted lord and master, but his former peers, now underlings, were swarming around him like animals at a salt lick in the Kalahari. It was humorous watching them all fawn over him and tell him just how fabulous he was.

66 *I cut it off in a snit.* 99

"Trey, it's about time," the creepy dark-haired woman cooed. Then she turned to Kiyoko and said, "Ki, if you had only explained what was happening, I would have understood of course. I didn't mean to come down so hard on you."

Yeah, you did, "Ki" thought, picking up her water glass and taking a drink as people pumped her hand and air-kissed her, telling her what a wonderful opportunity this was for her. Getting tribute was not a totally new experience—you couldn't be a crazy-cat Katsuda and not have enjoyed the spoils of privilege, to be blunt but, hopefully, not snotty—but it was still very sweet.

Through the craziness, Trey gestured for her to follow him out of the room. He moved fast and fluid, the leader of the pack, as he caught up with Bishop. Delia was yammering into her headset. Mel was looking a little overwhelmed. Maybe worrying about the future of print journalism.

"Now what, master?" Kiyoko asked him.

"Now we'll schmooze for a while, and then I have a brief meeting in Bishop's office," Trey said.

A chill fluttered through her. Maybe her staying Trey's intern was not a done deal. Two weeks from now, she would be leaving. Maybe he was too big a cheese to have an intern anymore. Maybe they would make her do *all* the filing from now on.

Or maybe I'll get to hang out with Belle Holder.

That would be beyond cool!

Kiyoko was in a fugue state by the time they cabbed it back and traipsed into Bishop's office. Kiyoko wasn't as young as she used to be; she couldn't stay up all night and then function well for an entire day. But she did manage to register her pleasure that she and Mel both were in the room. Delia rounded out their little party.

Bishop sat behind her desk. Trey sat in front of it, gesturing for Kiyoko to sit beside him. Mel kind of dithered.

Bishop's discriminating gaze swept over Kiyoko, pausing at the hood-purse in her lap. She said, "What on earth is that?"

Kiyoko lifted her chin. "The hood of my raincoat," she said. "I cut it off in a snit."

"Did you." Was she amused? Disdainful? Going to call all her friends and suggest they make some together?

Probably not.

But "did you" was the best Kiyoko was going to get.

Bishop said to Delia, "Tea. Trey?"

Kiyoko had to stifle herself from laughing aloud. She managed to sit down without incident, running a finger over the slickness of her purse as Trey requested mineral water. Kiyoko figured he had a fifty-gallon drum for a bladder.

Then Delia looked at her as if this were the single most humiliating moment in her life and said, "Would you like something, Kiyoko?"

Delia has to be nice to me. I'm movin' on up! "Sure," she said brightly. Then, at a look from Bishop, took it down. "Yes, thank you. Coffee. Strong. Black."

Mel was not included in the round-robin. She said to Delia, "I'll help you," which to Kiyoko's mind was a deft way of handling the situation.

"You will stay," Bishop informed her. "She'll have tea," she told Delia.

Delia nodded silently and left the room.

"So. Trey." Bishop leaned forward like they were best girlfriends and Trey had good gossip. "Are we happy?"

"Yes," he said. "We are happy."

"Fine. The attorney's office phoned and said they were messengering over the contracts with that rider you asked for." She turned to Kiyoko. "Exciting times, eh, Miss Katsuda?"

"Absolutely," Kiyoko said.

"The last two weeks before you're gone, and you girls get to watch a player in action." Bishop chuckled heartily, and Mel and Kiyoko traded a look. Bishop was enjoying this.

"It was cool," Kiyoko told her.

Bishop regarded her stonily. "'Cool.' That's what you have to say about it?"

"English is not my native language," Kiyoko said without shame. Bishop hated apologies. Kiyoko had figured out that much.

Bishop settled in behind her desk. "Ms. Katsuda, Trey is still head of Entertainment for the time being, but we're going to offload some of his duties onto Belle Holder. Including, to a large extent, you."

Kiyoko nodded. Her foot began to tap. Mel looked like she was going to keel over in a dead faint.

"So, you'll report to Trey *and* Belle," Bishop went on. "You'll be having a working breakfast with her on Friday."

"Is that when I'll get my assignment?" Kiyoko blurted.

"Oh, so you want one?" Bishop asked coolly. The lady definitely had an edge.

"Kiyoko's eager to prove herself," Trey said.

Bishop's cold-ray vision landed on her new Electronic Content dude. Not big with the warm fuzzies, Top Diva. She sniffed the way Liv might and cocked her head as she studied Kiyoko.

"I was under the impression that perhaps Ms. Katsuda was more interested in having a good time than doing good work," she said.

Though it was a total body blow, Kiyoko stepped

"Nothing I do is going to be good enough for her."

up. "I know you got that impression somehow, and I'm . . . that's the wrong impression. I really want to show you what I can do before I am outta here." She smiled hopefully.

"This is *Flirt* magazine, not an episode of *The Apprentice*," Bishop retorted.

Kiyoko was determined to remain unstung, but the truth was, with the no-sleep and the vast amounts of caffeine and—*yow!*—the sudden, pounding headache, she was beginning to hurt.

She licked her lips and said carefully, "I would like a chance, Bi—Ms. Bishop."

"Very well. I'll leave that to Trey and Belle to work out. But of course I reserve the right to veto it." She looked at Trey. "Do you have something for her to do this afternoon?"

"Plenty," he replied.

"Good." She looked at Kiyoko. "Go do it."

She was being dismissed. Kiyoko was bewildered. She thought she was staying for the meeting. Had she said something wrong? Had Bishop decided to talk to Trey about her?

Trey said smoothly, "We didn't have our Spotteds session today at lunch, Kiyoko. Please burn a CD for each of the department heads along with a little note explaining that they only need to read starting from where I made a notation."

"Yes, my liege," Kiyoko said automatically, then wondered if that was too flip for the new, improved, more important Trey. "My liege, sir," she muttered, and scrambled out of her chair.

"Let me see your purse again," Bishop demanded, stretching out her hand.

Obediently, Kiyoko handed it over.

Bishop held it with both hands, examining it and turning it over. "This is repulsive."

Kiyoko flashed her a lopsided grin. "Yeah. Not my best work."

Wordlessly, Bishop handed the purse back to her. Then she said to Mel, "Melanie, I downloaded some copy to your computer. I want you to see what you can do with it."

Melanie sat up straighter, as if aware that she, too, was now being shut out of whatever she had been brought in there to discuss.

"I'll need it back in an hour."

"Yes, Ms. Bishop."

Kiyoko waited for her mate at the door. Just as she was about to push it open, Delia bustled in with a tray of beverages, just like a glorified waitress. In the center stood a small white China teapot.

"Thank you," Kiyoko said breezily, picking up her coffee cup. "Mel, you had tea?" She quickly poured Mel a cup of tea and handed it to her.

Then she and Mel swept out into the hall.

The door clicked shut.

Kiyoko rolled her eyes and said, "Why does she have to be such an empress all the bloody time?"

"Okay, time out. You are overtired," Mel said, shushing her with her hands. "Go to your desk and do what Trey told you to do."

Kiyoko crossed her arms across her chest, slouching like a spoiled American. "Why should I bother, Mel? Her mind is made up about me. Nothing I do is going to be good enough for her."

"Kiyoko Katsuda, I can't believe what I'm hearing! Defeatist attitude from *you*?" Mel frowned and put her hands on her hips. She looked so fiercely Amazonian that Kiyoko almost started laughing.

"You're right. Launch the torpedoes and full steam ahead," Kiyoko said gamely. She made a fist and punched the air, mugging for her friend. "You gringos just adore the underdog, don't you?"

"Kiyoko, it's not a battle," Mel told her. "You need to get a better vibe going with her. Don't be so confrontational."

Kiyoko's mouth dropped open. "Mel, are you out of your mind? *Of course* it's a battle. Business is war."

"But we're not *in* business," Mel argued. "We're interns. I want to be a writer. What do you want to be?"

"Kiyoko," Kiyoko retorted. "I want to be myself."

"Then go be yourself at your desk," Mel said, giving her a little push. "Do the job Trey gave you as well as you can, then go home and get some sleep, and then we'll work on your music." She grinned at her friend. "You're going to present your material to that Sakamoto guy *and* meet Belle Holder! I would do anything to be at your power breakfast. Belle is our generation's Tama Janowitz."

"That's so nice. And obscure," Kiyoko drawled. She covered her mouth as another yawn escaped.

Mel was about to launch. "Tama Janowitz is—"

"Not the person who will boot me if I screw things up this afternoon," Kiyoko said, heading her friend off at the pass of a long explanation. "Tell me about her tonight? I'll go route Spotteds. Sounds like big game hunting, eh, what? Cheerio, lad!"

She went back to her desk, burned the CDs, routed them, and then drummed her fingers on her desk for a few seconds before she checked her cell. Calls and text messages. Matteo, Spider, Miko.

Spider told her about a fun new Korean restaurant with kimchee ice cream. She texted back and told him that Belle Holder was joining *Flirt*. Spider was extremely impressed.

Matteo taught her how to say "My life is filled with thrills!" in Afrikaans. She had no idea why he was suddenly so interested in Afrikaans. It didn't matter why. It was just cool that he was.

MATTeO: Might have kewl bday surprise!

An hour flashed past before she knew it. She was stunned. She had forgotten to turn off the voice-mail system again!

I have got to do something workish!

Rubbing her sleepy-dirt eyes, she hurried into Trey's office to retrieve his "While You Were Abducted by Aliens" list of things to do. There was a stickie on his clock that hadn't been there before the lunch. It read: *Drinks to celebrate? Demetria.*

Whoa, she's not wasting any time, Kiyoko thought.

Then someone delivered flowers. More flowers. A bottle of Cristal Champagne. The tributes were pouring in. Trey could make some serious money on eBay with all the stuff.

There really wasn't much on Trey's list that she could do herself. She verified a couple of phone numbers, and returned a couple of calls from other departments. But in every case, what the caller wanted was something only Trey knew about.

She drummed her fingers. She wanted to prove herself to Bishop, but she didn't have anything to do.

And then she realized she could work on her music for Matsumoto and Kanno. For the love of the divine Buddha, she was sitting in the Entertainment division of *Flirt*. Surely they had musical software programs up the wazoo!

She opened the applications section of her desktop and hunted around. *Banzai!* Total gold! She opened some apps and perused them, blessing her grandmother a million times over for insisting that she and her brother and sister take music lessons.

She located a pair of headphones and plugged them in. Then she looked at a few web episodes of *Tokyo Goddess,* a long-running Matsumoto-Kanno series on Japanese TV. On a fansite, she listened over and over to different samples of Kanno's music, especially "Tadao's Theme." Then she replicated the melody, orchestrating it a dozen ways. Jiro Kanno used those cool synthesized choral voices and lots of strings. She tweaked her composition, retaining only a few note sequences as she wove a new sound around Kanno's essential Tadao core.

She hit playback and listened hard. Pretty good. She worked on it some more.

After a while she glanced at the time/date readout on her computer. It was six. What was Trey's deal? He rarely made her stay this late.

She experimented a little bit more.

> **66 *I have got to do something workish!* 99**

Six thirty. She was so tired, she took off the headset and laid her head down on her desk and let herself doze off. Just for a sec. Maybe two secs . . .

"Kiyoko?" It was Trey.

She looked up at him blearily and mumbled, "Sorry. Long night. I mean, day."

It was so *quiet*. No music. She looked around. They were alone, no other employees hustling and bustling. Most of the lights were off; an overhead shone down on Trey's well-groomed head like a halo. "What time is it?"

"You didn't check the messages after you left Ms. Bishop's office," he said.

"No, I did," she began, but she realized she had only checked the ones she had written down before they'd left for lunch and the ones in her e-mail in-box. And on her cell phone. And then she had put on the headphones.

You bloody moron!

"I didn't know you were still here. I've been with Ms. Bishop all this time. We've been putting out fires. Seems some people are a tad upset about my promotion."

"Of course they are," she said, pulling herself together. "I was furious when I didn't get the Fashion beat, but . . . I'm so glad I'm here instead," she said quickly, pulling a save.

"I left you a voice-mail telling you that you could go home," he said. He added, "It's almost eleven."

"What?" She bolted upright. "That's my curfew!"

He exhaled impatiently. "Well, if you'd checked the messages . . ."

"Oh, God," she wailed. "Please, Trey, *please*, can you call Emma and explain?"

He sighed. "All right. What's the number?"

She rattled off Emma's number—she had it memorized—and tapped her foot while Trey made the call.

He was cool. He covered for her, explaining that he had kept Kiyoko busy all evening. Emma forgave.

Kiyoko said, "Thank you, Trey, thank you!" She grabbed her purse. "I'm gone!"

She leaped into a cab.

This cannot count against me with Emma, she thought as Sammy the doorman gave her a wave and tapped his watch. She trudged wearily past him with barely a *"Komban wa."*

She took the lift up, tensing for a dressing-down. But the loft was dark and silent, except for the light beside the sofa. There was a plate there, and a brownie and a glass of milk.

Warning: Carob said the note, in Mel's handwriting.

Grateful for Mel's kindness, Kiyoko wolfed down the brownie as she headed for the bathroom. She changed, brushed her teeth, and tiptoed into her room. For a second she couldn't remember the way to her bed.

Her cell phone vibrated. She checked it; she had a text message.

SPIDER_K: MISSED U!

She smiled grimly and put her purse on her desk. Her bed felt even better than the night before.

Then she reached inside and pulled out Shinichiro Matsumoto's card. He was leaving town on Friday, and she had nothing to show him.

Tomorrow is only Thursday, she told herself. *And Thursday is the new today.*

She set the alarm for four thirty and climbed into bed.

She was gone in sixty seconds.

chapter seven

Kiyoko meant well.

She got up at five, not four thirty, but she was so tired that she went back to bed at six; and as a result, she was late for work. Trey had a million kabillion things for her to do to get ready for Belle Holder, whose first day would be tomorrow. She had no downtime to herself all day, not even lunch. After work, she was going to go straight back to the loft to work on "the Kanno Project," but because she so very much needed to decompress, she agreed to go to Noodletown with Mel, Alexa, and Liv and her boyfriend, Eli.

It was a pretty decent and very inexpensive Chinese restaurant in the Village, decorated with all kinds of art depicting people eating noodles. They ordered all kinds of dishes with soft noodles and crunchy noodles, plus *mu shu* shrimp, which was one of Kiyoko's comfort foods.

The waiter was adorable, and she cheered up when he kept coming by to refill their teapot. What a hottie. He wanted her so much.

Then she got a text message from Matteo:

MATTeO: KikO! Bday surprise a go!

"Oh, my God," Alexa breathed, covering her cheeks with her hands. Her eyes glittered. "He's going to propose!"

Kiyoko nearly sprayed tea all over the table. "Bloody hell, Alexa! Are you mad?"

"It would be so romantic," Alexa cooed. "We could be your bridesmaids."

"I am sixteen years old. Matteo will be eighteen in twenty days. I seriously doubt marriage is on the lad's feverish brain." She gestured to Mel. "Mel will be the first of us to marry, I'm sure. Hippies marry young."

"Hippies didn't marry at all," Mel retorted. "I think. I'm a postmodern hippie."

Liv smiled and drank tea.

"He's probably going to give you a nice present to welcome you home," Alexa said.

Kiyoko shook her head. "Alexa, remember: He's in Los Angeles now, staying with his aunt until the term begins."

"Oh, I'm sorry." Alexa sighed. "How tragic."

"No." Kiyoko shrugged. "We're very long distance. But we're used to it. We text, call, IM . . . it's the next best thing to being there."

"But it's not the same," Alexa argued.

"But almost," Kiyoko said. "We'll probably meet up during the hols." At their looks, she said, "Winter break, whatever you call it."

"That's months from now," Alexa argued. "I don't know what Ben and I are going to do after the summer ends." Ben was her brand-new New York boyfriend, and she was totally into him.

"Alexa, if it's working for them, that's all that matters," Mel said. "People have all different kinds of relationships."

"Spoken like a true Northern Californian," Kiyoko said, stirring her tea with the end of her chopstick. "It works." She slugged back her tea with a satisfied sigh. "Now, I've got to go back to the loft and work on my music." She ran her fingers through her long black hair and shook it out. "I haven't come up with much of *anything*."

"You haven't had any time," Mel said loyally. "Let's get the check and go home and you can work. We'll help you."

Alexa and Liv nodded.

Kiyoko beamed at the lot of them. "You're always helping me. Thank you."

"What are friends for?" Mel asked. "Besides, I'm counting on you to introduce me to Belle. Tomorrow's your breakfast, right?"

"Maybe she can help you with your music for Jiro Kanno," Eli suggested. Eli had known Kiyoko for a few years and he was well familiar with her musical aspirations.

"Wow," Kiyoko said, suddenly very shy at the

thought of approaching such a famous person about her music thing. "I don't know."

"Maybe that could be your article," Mel said, seized with sudden inspiration. "'How I Wrote Music for the Matsumoto-Kanno Team.'"

"Rock!" cried Alexa.

"That would be brill," Liv agreed.

As they walked back to the loft, Kiyoko worked out some melodies in her head. Then, when they got home, she powered up her laptop and told the girls she needed to do some research—nothing they could help with. They hung around for a while, but eventually they drifted out of the room. Gen was in the main area of the loft, which was a blessing. Kiyoko did not need her snide reactions during her work session.

Settling in, she went on the Net and found a portion of *Castle of Hildago*, the Matsumoto-Kanno anime feature that had premiered in Tokyo last summer. She listened hard to the music cues, timing them with the clock function on her computer screen. Most of them were under a minute. How many of her own should she create? How long should they be?

"Kiyoko?" Liv called softly from the doorway. She was wearing black velour sweats and scuffies. "It's Nick's birthday. Would you like to take a break? Emma made a wonderful New York cheesecake."

I'll go out just for a minute, Kiyoko promised herself. *Be sociable. Have some cake and get back in here.*

> **The nutty creature had a girlfriend, so that had taken care of any hope of a summer romance between him and Mel. But a girl could still look ...**

She followed Liv into the loft proper. Emma, Gen, and Charlotte were gathered around the rectangular dinner table, with Nick at the head in front of a small pile of wrapped packages. He was wearing a Burger King crown, a sleeveless T-shirt, and a pair of baggy shorts. There was paint on his tanned shoulders and biceps. The splotches looked like postmodern tattoos.

Mel is going to love this, she thought. Mel had crushed on Nick earlier in the summer, and no wonder. He was so adorable. The nutty creature had a girlfriend, so that had taken care of any hope of a summer romance between him and Mel. But a girl could still look . . .

"Mel and Alexa went to get some soda," Emma said as if she could read her mind. "We're waiting until they get back to have the cheesecake."

"*And* open presents," Nick said, rubbing his hands together.

"Wait until you see what *I* got you," Gen told him. The poor girl just never gave up, even though she'd known Nick for years. Meaning, she also knew his girlfriend.

"No fair," Liv protested. "You should have told us it was

your birthday, Nick. I would have gotten you a gift, too."

"Nick's like Van Gogh," Gen interjected, sounding proprietary. "If you give him something, he's going to sell it on eBay to buy paint."

"So, what, did you buy him paint?" Kiyoko sniped.

Gen snickered. Perhaps to smooth things over, Emma looked around and said, "I wonder what's taking them so long."

Yeah, Kiyoko thought as she pulled out a chair and sat down. *I hope they show soon. I need to get back to my music.*

Kiyoko told Emma, "Japanese people are crazy about cheesecake. The best cheesecake I've ever had was in a restaurant near my grandmother's house on Hokkaido."

"Really?" Emma raised her brows. "Did you happen to get the recipe? I'm a cheesecake maven."

"Her cheesecake is so good, she thought about starting a catering business," Nick said.

"Well, I didn't get the recipe exactly," Kiyoko said. "But they told me the secret was adding some superfine sugar." She thought a moment. "That's what you call it in English, right? Superfine?"

Emma nodded. Then she batted at Nick, who had picked up a DVD-shaped package wrapped in balloon paper and was tearing at the Scotch-taped end with his thumbnail. "Stop that!" she said. "Presents after cake!'

"It's *Forbearance,*" he said, thrilled. He tore off the rest of the gift wrap. "With the deleted scenes." He skimmed the back. "Thanks, Mom. Oh, wow. They included a suite of the score by Alastair McGinnis." He looked excitedly at Kiyoko, waving the DVD box at her. "You know about that, music intern? They paid McGinnis a million dollars to do the soundtrack. Then the studio scrapped it and started over. The director was furious. He almost walked."

"I never heard of that," Kiyoko said, intrigued. "Did he get to keep the money?"

Nick nodded. "But the studio owned it, so he couldn't do anything with it."

"That totally sucks," Kiyoko said. "That's unjust."

Nick tapped the box. "The suite's just twelve minutes long. Let's check it out. We won't watch the movie until the girls get back." He carried the DVD to the big-screen TV and popped open the state-of-the-art Sony DVD player.

Everyone grouped around the couch and got comfy as he aimed the remote at the player. The DVD selection menu showed a French countryside, a horse, and a man's silhouette. Nick clicked over to "Special Features" and then to "McGinnis Suite."

Full, lush music hummed from the speakers.

"It sounds like Jiro Kanno," Kiyoko told the others, feeling both a fillip of excitement and a rush of anxiety. She hadn't told anyone but Mel, Liv, and Alexa about her meeting with Matsumoto and Kanno. She didn't want to jinx herself, and she didn't need any goading or teasing from anyone. Gen would have nothing nice or encouraging to say.

Kiyoko rose from the couch to go back to work just

as Mel and Alexa burst through the lift door in a shower of giggles. They were each carrying a brown grocery bag.

"Never go to the store when you're hungry!" Alexa said gaily, charging into the room. "You will *not* believe all the things we bought!"

"Or who we found!" Mel said.

A tall, dark-skinned guy bounded out of the lift. A beautiful red-haired girl was holding onto his arm.

"Spider!" Kiyoko cried, rushing up to him.

"Darling girl!" he said, spinning her around. "I heard these two ladies calling each other Mel and Alexa, and I knew they had to be your friends."

"Oh, you are Sherlock Holmes!" Kiyoko cried.

"I am," Spider agreed. "And this is Chara. She just finished modeling with Miko in London."

"Get out," Kiyoko said. "What's my sister up to?"

"No good at all," Chara said, wrinkling her nose. "She's tarting up, to tell you the truth."

She, Kiyoko, and Spider cracked up.

"You were only supposed to buy soda," Gen chastised Mel. "We've been waiting forever."

"Look, I'm trying to compose some music," Kiyoko said. "Come and listen?"

"Love to," Spider said.

Then Emma cleared her throat. Oops, no male guests.

"I think the Starbucks is still open," Kiyoko said, ticking a glance toward Emma to see if that was all right.

66 *This is a mistake, Kiyoko thought.* 99

"Will you be offended if we leave before cake?" she asked Nick.

Nick shook his head no.

"Great. I'll get my laptop."

She fetched it, said happy birthday once more, and popped into the lift with Spider and Chara. She gave Sammy a wave and he waved back. Then they sailed into the Starbucks and commandeered a sofa and an overstuffed chair.

"What's this for?" Spider asked as he flopped onto the sofa with Chara.

"I'm going to see Jiro Kanno," she said, taking the chair.

Spider and Chara looked at each other. They obviously didn't know who he was.

"It's for anime," she said.

"Oh." Spider chuckled. "These Japanese cartoons she likes."

"I know what anime is, Spider," Chara said indignantly. "I'm not stupid."

"Let me get us all something to drink," Spider said, getting to his feet.

Chara looked at Kiyoko. She bent forward and wrapped her hands around her knees. "How exciting, making music."

This is a mistake, Kiyoko thought. *I'm not going to get anything done.*

As Spider returned, she closed her laptop and rose.

"I'm sorry, guys, but I have to get this done tonight," she said. "I'd like to see you, but—"

"Whoa, who is this? It's not Kiyoko," Spider protested. "You're a party girl, girl!"

"Not tonight," she told them, with a little smile. "Sorry."

"It's okay," Spider said. "It was lovely to see you for a bit. Now, go."

She did. She went back through the lobby, waving at Sammy again, and let herself in the lift.

Should I get as close to Jiro Kanno as I can or go in an entirely different direction? she wondered, suddenly very unsure. She felt herself break out in a cold sweat. She had stage fright.

As the lift doors opened into the Flirt-cave, she saw everyone gathered around the telly, bursting en masse into loud guffaws.

She wandered into the room and stood behind the couch. She had never seen *Forbearance*. It was a French farce that had done very well in Japan. She found herself translating the French rather than reading the English.

"Is everyone in Europe a rutting bunny?" a little boy asked his mother.

"No, darling, just we French."

The entire room cascaded into gales of laughter.

Kiyoko shifted her weight and crossed her arms. Obviously she'd missed a lot. Oh! The setting had changed to England. There was the bridle path she and Miko used to ride down. And there were the Mews!

"Oh! See that building?" Liv cried. "Sting used to own that. It's in Hampstead Heath."

Liv lived in Hampstead Heath part of the year. Kiyoko had friends there but had never been to Liv's house.

The little boy turned out to be the son of the rich man's mistress and her lover. Kiyoko laughed along with the others when he showed up at the man's funeral in a bunny suit.

And then the credits were rolling.

She blanched. She hadn't meant to stay for the duration.

"Cheesecake!" Emma cried. She was placing candles into the custard-colored surface of the cake. "Let's sing 'Happy Birthday.'"

They all sang together, Alexa singing "*Cumpleaños Felíz.*" Nick blew out the candles, and his mother cut the cake. Mel passed out pieces while Alexa popped open the cans of soda.

Kiyoko wolfed down her cake, and carried a can of diet back into her lair.

She sat back down at her laptop, sipping and replaying her melodies. That one wasn't bad. That one was bloody horrid.

She slumped.

"How is it going?" Mel asked from the doorway.

Kiyoko pulled a long face. "I suck."

"No, you don't," loyal Mel assured her. She came into the room and stood beside Kiyoko. "Play them for me."

Kiyoko lined them up and hit Play. They warbled and wobbled, and Kiyoko winced at how awful they were.

"I like 'em," Mel said; and Kiyoko knew for sure that there was nothing Mel could do to help her. If she liked these monstrosities, then she knew absolutely zed about music.

"Thanks," she said, meaning it. Mel was a dear, kind girl. No sense dissing her for being enthusiastic on a friend's behalf. "I'm going to finish up now," she added, hinting that she'd like to be alone.

"Okay. Let me know if you need anything," Mel said sweetly.

Kiyoko nodded. She decided to Google some more sites and see if there was any bit of music Kanno had done lately that she had not heard. She came across a downloaded version of *Tendai Vampire Z* and watched for a little while, stopping when she realized she hadn't been listening to the music at all.

I'll get inspired tomorrow after breakfast with Belle Holder, Kiyoko promised herself. *Music is my thing.*

She set the alarm for five A.M.

And slept right through it.

ⓖ   ⓖ   ⓖ   ⓖ

"Kiyoko! Wake up!" Mel cried. "You're late!"

Disaster! Predicament! Tragedy!

But . . . salvageable, yes?

Kiyoko was all nerves as she dressed for her breakfast at Caffe Reggio with Belle Holder, but she kept herself together. She grabbed a ruffly silk blouse, a short, ruched black spandex skirt embroidered with heads of the Japanese '50s monster Mothra, and a pair of Japanese geta, which were essentially platform sandals. She applied a few random stick-ons to her toenails, mostly of kanji—the writing system made of ancient Chinese characters that was used for most printed material in Japan. Her kanji represented "luck," "fortune," and "longevity."

> **She so did not want to get into it with Gen this morning.**

"Do you think you can get her autograph?" Charlotte asked Kiyoko as Kiyoko grabbed a slice of bacon off Alexa's plate and chased it with some orange juice.

"Oh, please," Gen said, sneering at her hapless minion. "If you really want it, I can get it for you. Aunt Jo will probably have her sign a stack of pictures to donate to charity."

"Oh. Cool," Charlotte replied.

Kiyoko couldn't imagine the dignified Josephine Bishop doing such a thing, but she didn't voice her opinion. She so did not want to get into it with Gen this morning.

"Have fun," Mel said as she, Alexa, and Kiyoko spilled out of the lift, through the lobby, and into the bright New York morning. The muggy heat clung to her, reminding Kiyoko of Japan.

"Tell her we are her biggest fans," Alexa added, giving Kiyoko a wave as she and Mel headed for the subway. Kiyoko was going to walk.

Kiyoko pulled her sunglasses out of her purse, a vintage straw cylinder she had chosen to tie in with her geta. Now, on her way, she was pumped. She dwelled on the bright side: She had fantastic friends; Caffe Reggio was a famous Village landmark; and Belle Holder was a bona fide celeb. And little tunes were playing in her head—her own anime soundtrack! What could be a better start to a brand-new day? Everything would work out.

Here was proof: Possibly the cutest bike messenger Kiyoko had ever seen pedaled in slow-motion alongside her. He was wearing a T-shirt and bike shorts that revealed ultracut thighs. She stared openly at him, and he rang his bell at her.

She smiled at him.

"Cool shoes," he said, gesturing to her geta.

She threw back her hair. "Thanks."

"Do you live around here?"

"For the moment."

Then she looked ahead, saw an overturned trash can in his path, and bellowed, *"Abunai!"* Which meant, "Look out!"

So maybe Japanese, not Portuguese, was her native language after all.

He slammed on his brakes with a mighty squeal, stopping mere inches from the trash can. "You care," he said as he put down his foot to steady himself. He was a bit sweaty. Kiyoko thought that was hot.

"I care," she agreed, grinning at him as she walked on. He *clinged* his bicycle bell at her again and she walked off with a spring in her step. *Clack, clack, clack.*

Then she reached Caffe Reggio on MacDougal Street and her heart sped up as she scanned for the famous journo. The exterior was wood painted the color of iodized copper, and most of the outside tables were occupied with people in summery business attire drinking coffee, reading the paper, and talking or texting on phones. Kiyoko felt another fluttery bit of excitement—*I'm part of this!*—and started looking for the very famous person she was about to meet.

"Hey, Kiyoko?"

Waving her hand, Belle Holder sat at a table with three chairs beside the entrance.

Kiyoko waved back and clacked toward her.

"Hey, *o-hayo gozaimasu*," Belle greeted her in excellent Japanese.

"*O-hayo gozaimasu.* Good morning," Kiyoko said back, unable to stop herself from executing a bow. The impulse was hard-wired into Japanese people. "You speak Japanese."

"Yeah."

Belle's hair was very blond and very short, and she had enormous blue eyes and a tiny mouth. She was petite and thin—the word "scrawny" came to mind—and much shorter than she appeared on TV and in photographs. She was dressed in stretchy black pants, a vintage Rolling Stones T-shirt, and scuffed boots à la Johnny Depp. A red thread Kabbalah bracelet was wound around her left wrist, and her right eyebrow was pierced.

"So, how's it hangin'?" Belle asked; then her cell phone trilled and she said, "Sec." She took it. "Yeah." Then she started swearing like a sailor. Kiyoko was fascinated. Matteo had been teaching her every English swear word he knew, but he was obviously an amateur. She sat with a master now, and she took mental notes.

Evidently someone had mixed up two photo captions on a piece Belle had already approved. Belle wanted him fired.

"And you tell that so-called 'editor' that he can just kiss my butt," she continued as Trey walked up.

"Hi," Belle said to him; then into the phone, "I'll catch you later, okay, Chachi? Who loves you, mmm? Kiss. Get him gone for me? Thank you, babe."

She disconnected and set the phone on the table.

Trey looked hot, as in adorable. He had on nice trousers and a silk T-shirt; he smelled like a soapy shower and Kiyoko wondered if he had gone out with Demetria.

"Hey, Trey." Belle stuck out her hand.

"Belle. Such a pleasure." He had a copy of *Rolling Stone* with him, which he fwapped onto the table. He said, "Fantastic article on Mick." Sure enough, there was a picture of Mick Jagger on the cover wearing a white T-shirt that said *Belle*.

"Oh, God, I don't know how we pulled that one together," Belle grumbled good-naturedly. "I was freaking out."

A waiter came, and the trio placed their order.

Then Trey gestured to Belle and said to the waiter, "I'll have what she's having," and the two grown-ups chuckled. Kiyoko didn't know why, and her ignorance must have been showing, because Trey explained, "That's from a movie called *When Harry Met Sally.*"

"I know," Kiyoko blurted, then realized she wasn't fooling them and said, "Actually, I don't."

"God, to be so young again," Belle murmured. "It would suck." She cracked up at her own humor. Then she launched into a funny story about interviewing Alicia Keys. Kiyoko debated telling her about Vlad Moscow and decided against it. Best foot forward and all that.

Their food came. They discussed it. The lox was good. The bagels were fresh. What about the rumor that Miss Thing was going to stop touring? J's Podcast, what a disaster! Kiyoko nodded along, but she was following very little of it.

"So, congratulations on the Electronic Content gig," Belle said to Trey without pausing for breath. "That's sweet. I found out the coolest thing," Belle went on. "My assignment editor at *Wired* went to Brown with Jo Bishop's nephew. How about that?"

Trey grunted.

She looked at Kiyoko. Kiyoko grunted.

"Brown is a university here in America," Trey said.

"I know," Kiyoko replied. And she did. "I've done a lot of research on the U.S. And also lived here before." *How lame does that sound?*

The plates went away. Everyone had coffee-drink refills. By then they were on thirds. Kiyoko was getting jittery from so much caffeine.

"So, I understand that you get an assignment in order to complete your internship," Belle announced as she dumped one, two, three, four packets of raw sugar into her cup. "Ms. Bishop suggested I talk to you about some ideas. That sound good?"

Kiyoko nodded, beyond thrilled. Belle Holder was about to talk to her about her big showpiece!

"A gig for an intern." Belle looked at Trey for pointers as she stirred. Then she lifted her oversize latte with both hands and chugged it down.

"Earlier in the summer, Kiyoko made a killer list of bands she guessed would hit the big time. Cutting-edge sounds. Maybe she could do a piece on one of them," Trey ventured.

"I'm um, I could do it on Matsumoto and Kanno," Kiyoko said. "I met them and—"

"How about doing one on freeback?" Belle asked.

Kiyoko's lips parted. *Freeback?* Freeback was a musical style where the backbeat time signature shifted—from three-four to four-four, for example. Or four-four to five-four, and back again. It had potentially been a neat idea, but unfortunately, no one had gone much past covering old songs against the new beat. It was like the very worst of disco parading as something special . . . and it wasn't. It was boring and predictable after you heard two or three songs.

And for whatever unbelievable reason it had become trendy, it was mercifully over.

"You know what it is, right?" Belle asked, and before Kiyoko could answer, she settled her huge cup in its saucer and leaned forward eagerly, as if she were about to tell her two best friends some very dishy secret. "I really think it's here to stay."

Kiyoko glanced at Trey for assistance. Maybe this was some kind of test to see if Kiyoko was keeping up with the musical landscape. But Trey was concentrating on stirring a cube of sugar into his sea of coffee.

Kiyoko's foot began tapping. She took a hefty swallow of cappuccino and said, "Um, I think the world has moved on."

Belle blinked. "Well, you're wrong. Jenny Stewart is recording an entire freeback album right now."

Yeah, well, that just proves my point. Jenny Stewart has been committing career suicide for the last two albums, Kiyoko

> ## **Kiyoko managed to alter the dimensions of her frozen smile without cracking her face in half.**

wanted to say, but she took another jolt of cappuccino while she pondered what on earth she was supposed to do here.

Trey said, "I'm sorry. I have a call I need to take." He slipped on his headset and left the table.

Do you hate me? Kiyoko silently called after him.

"I'm thinking around eight hundred to a thousand words and two or three random pictures to go with it," Belle concluded. She leaned back in her chair again and crossed her arms, looking very pleased with herself. A little silver stud in her nose caught the light. She was like the anti-Tinkerbell.

"Pictures of . . . ?" *The three people in the known universe who still listen to freeback?*

"I'll leave that up to you," Belle said, grinning, as she slung her booted ankle across her knee. She gave Kiyoko a look. "Of course, if you're not interested . . . I thought you'd want to have a piece on the new *Flirt* network. This would totally work."

"Yes, yes," Kiyoko said eagerly, hoping her big smile did not look like a silent scream of protest. "Of course I do."

"Cool," Belle enthused, clapping her hands together. "I'll clear it with Ms. Bishop. You only have a little while until you leave, right? So how about you turn in a draft Monday? That'll give us a full work week to polish it into a final." She looked up. "Trey, looks like we've got her set," she informed him as he came back to the table. "I'll check with the boss, but I'm willing to bet she'll approve it."

"Faboo, you." Without sitting down, Trey raised his cup to Belle and Kiyoko both. "That's great, Kiyoko. I know you've been waiting for this. Thanks, B. Listen, I have to take off. If you two have more to discuss—"

"No, no, we're done," Belle assured him. "We'll go back with you to the office. Kiyoko can start working on her piece." She wrinkled her nose like an indulgent aunt. "Find some good clubs to check out. The most important one is Café Endless. You *have* to go there. Friday nights are always crazy there."

"Her curfew is midnight on the weekends," Trey said, humiliating her beyond the depths of humiliation.

"Oh?" Belle looked disbelieving.

"It's the truth," Trey assured her as he picked up his sunglasses and put them on. "She's only sixteen, after all."

Belle shrugged. "At sixteen, I had dropped out of high school and was bumming across China. Not that *you* should." She sighed. "Well, it is what it is. Kiyoko strikes me as the resourceful type." She grinned at Kiyoko, and Kiyoko managed to alter the dimensions of her frozen smile without cracking her face in half.

KIYOKO'S BLOG:

I know that someone will send this in:

Dear *Flirt*,
    I have been a loyal subscriber for three hundred years, but now I must ask you never to send your rag to me again. That article on freeback by Kiyoko Katsuda sucked hugely! It was the worst thing you have ever published. I am sticking to *Teen Vogue* and *Jane* from now on.
Your former fan,
Haley in San Diego
P.S. I have deleted flirt.com from my bookmarks.

    This is a nightmare. I have waited all summer to power on, and this is what I get?
    Jiro Kanno is my only hope now. Which is a pretty big hope!
    MOOD: UPBEAT.
    MUSIC: "Don't Worry, Be Happy" by that guy.

chapter eight

Trey, Belle, and Kiyoko cabbed it back to the *Flirt* offices. Trey had to peel off to see Quinn. Belle, walking with Kiyoko into the Entertainment sector, suddenly decided that Kiyoko needed to track down the reclusive guitarist, Mahlon Lumbumba, for an interview. There was no more discussion of her locating cool freeback clubs.

And no chance for her to work on some more music for Matsumoto and Kanno.

After working feverishly until nearly two P.M. with nothing to eat and hardly even taking time to pee, Kiyoko triumphantly marched to Belle's makeshift office—which consisted mostly of boxes—with a juicy tidbit pried from none other than Mr. Lumbumba's publicist: Mahlon was going to jam at Stinkers on Saturday around midnight. Kiyoko had even Googled Stinkers in case Belle needed to know where it was.

"She's gone," said Hilda. "She left at noon."

"What?" Kiyoko cried, dumbfounded. "But she told me . . . she said . . ."

"She'll be back Monday morning," Hilda informed her, in a tone that implied that Kiyoko was totally out of the loop because she hadn't known, while *she* was an up-and-comer destined for greater things. "I'm her secretary now," she added importantly.

"Did she leave a number to call her?" Kiyoko asked.

"Afraid not," Hilda said breezily.

Clenching her jaw, Kiyoko stomped back to her desk and typed Belle an "FYI" e-mail about Mahlon Lumbumba, using the standard address protocol: belle_h@flirt.com.

The mailer-daemon returned her message as undeliverable.

She tried the phone system. Belle didn't have a mailbox yet.

Then her own phone rang, and she grabbed it out of her purse.

MATTeO: HOLA!
KIYoKO!!!: GUTEN TAG!
MATTeO: How RU?
KIYoKO!!!: Big audition for Jiro
    Kanno!
MATTeO: LUCK!

"Kiyoko?" It was Trey, heading toward her desk with a shiny CD in his hand. Kiyoko disconnected and slipped her phone back into her purse at the same time that she squared her shoulders and beamed him a grateful smile. She was beyond overjoyed to see her old boss again.

"Mahlon Lumbumba is jamming at Stinkers tomorrow, and I don't know how to contact Belle," she said by way of greeting.

He gave her a quizzical look. "Okay." He perched on the edge of her desk.

"Belle asked me to find out. Only now she's gone, and I don't know how to tell her. She needed to know right away." *Or she said she did.* "She doesn't have an e-mail account here, and I tried to leave her a voice-mail and—"

"Whoa, Kiyoko, slow down."

She exhaled. "I'm sorry. It's just that . . ." She trailed off. She didn't want to whine to Trey about his replacement. How would that look? Like she couldn't handle having a new boss, that was how.

Trey nodded, examining the shiny CD surface and holding it up to the light.

"Belle told me Ms. Bishop cleared your piece. That's great," he said.

Kiyoko blinked. Belle had not mentioned it to *her.* Surely he knew how wrong it would be. Her one chance to show what she could do . . . She couldn't bear to see the expressions on the faces of Hiro and Miko when they read it. The pleasure Hiro would take in her humiliation. . . Miko's sympathy.

Then her *Flirt* line rang.

"Entertainment," she said, glancing up at Trey, who

> **" Then she took a breath and pulled out
> Matsumoto-san's card.
> Before she could stop herself,
> she dialed the number. "**

crossed his arms and waited to see who it was.

It was Bishop. "I'm sending all the interns to Central Park for the shoot this afternoon," the big boss informed her. "Jesse Greenfield is one of the foremost fashion photographers, and I want you girls to see her in action."

"Yes, Ms. Bishop," Kiyoko managed, but in truth she was freaking out anew. She was going to have to ditch it to get to her appointment.

"The limo leaves in half an hour." Bishop hung up.

Trey cocked his head. Kiyoko explained, "She wants me to go watch a photo shoot at Central Park."

He nodded. "Oh, right. Good." He smiled at her. "Later."

What could she do, be sick? She drummed her fingers on her desk.

Then she took a breath and pulled out Matsumoto-san's card. Before she could stop herself, she dialed the number. Hayeda-san answered.

"Would it be possible to delay our interview by one hour?" Kiyoko asked, shutting her eyes and wincing.

"*Sho-sho omachi, kudasai,*" Hayeda-san replied.

Please wait one minute.

She came back on the line. "That would be fine."

Kiyoko exhaled with relief. As usual, she had pulled it off. *Thank goodness.*

I'm going to knock their socks off, she thought.

⟟   ⟟   ⟟   ⟟

"My assignment sucks. But I have a couple of cool cues to play for Jiro Kanno," she said as she gobbled down the second of two hot dogs she had snagged at a cart bordering Central Park. She was sitting cross-legged on an enormous boulder near the sailboat pond. Mel was seated about a foot below her, writing on an old-fashioned steno pad. Kiyoko thought she looked cute, like Lois Lane.

Lynn and Alexa were the busiest of the busy as they chatted with Jesse Greenfield. Alexa was over the moon; the woman had studied with Helmut Newton.

A stone's throw away, four makeup artists were spray-painting three half-naked models—actually, they had on skimpy, flesh-colored bras and thongs—gray, brown, and black to make them look like rocks. Kiyoko had no idea why; the clothes they would be wearing were mostly red. She made no connections and frankly, she didn't care. Her freeback assignment sucked, and she wanted seven more hot dogs. She was starving.

"You're not wrong about your article, amiga," Alexa said as she stopped clicking away on her digital camera and reached for the Nikon with actual film inside it. She was in the zone, thoroughly enjoying herself by taking tons of pictures. Mel free-associating: *hard as rocks, loves me like a rock, rock on*.

"Gee, thanks," Kiyoko grumbled as she licked mustard off her fingers.

A few feet away, Liv helped with wardrobe. Racks of red, maroon, and burgundy dresses had been cut apart so they could be sewn onto the models after they were painted. Liv's hair was pulled back in a ponytail, and she had straight pins in her mouth. Closer to the action, Gen was scrutinizing the makeup application, and Charlotte, standing beside Gen, looked like she had no idea why she was there. Health and Fitness was such a lame beat.

"I can't believe Belle Holder came up with that," Alexa said. She turned to Mel. "You said she was jacked in."

"Freeback. Can you believe it?" Kiyoko stuck her finger in her mouth and made retching noises.

Rocks in her head, Mel wrote.

"I do not have rocks in my head," Kiyoko said, jabbing her finger at Mel's notepad. "I'm right. Am I right? Freeback is dead."

"It is not," Liv said, coming over to them as she jabbed the straight pins into a pin cushion that looked like a tomato. A gray velour tank and a silver cashmere scarf were draped over her arm. Rock colors, not red. Perhaps there had been a change in plans. "Freeback is very alive. I love it. Everyone loves it. My iPod nano is packed with it."

"No offense, Liv, but that doesn't surprise me," Kiyoko said offensively. She turned back to Mel. "And I can't believe you're using a pencil and paper. Aren't you part of the new electronic *Flirt* network, lad?"

"Chill, Kiyoko," Gen said, wandering over to the group. "You're just acting out because your life is going to pot."

"God, Gen," Alexa said.

Kiyoko scrambled to the top of the rock, pulling her legs up and resting her chin on her knees as she watched the models.

She said, "My music is going to rock those guys. You wait."

As if on cue, classical music started pumping out of speakers as the famous photographer directed her assistant in the positioning of freestanding lights and screens. Ms. Greenfield had told them all that she had had dental surgery that morning and not to talk to her.

Kiyoko said, "She wants me to go to Café Endless."

"Oh, that's a wonderful place!" Liv cried. "There's a brill DJ there most weekends. Maybe you could interview him for your piece."

Kiyoko moaned.

"Want to go there after this?" Liv asked. "We eat dinner there, start mingling."

"Well, here's the thing," Kiyoko said. "I've got to go to interview Matsumoto and Kanno in about three minutes."

"Right." Liv nodded.

"We'll distract the bosses," Alexa promised her. "You just wander off."

"Good luck," Mel said warmly. "Not that you need it."

Kiyoko winked at her and said, "You're the bomb, gringa!"

Charge!

⟲   ⟲   ⟲   ⟲

It was pushing four forty when Kiyoko hailed a cab to the building where Shinichiro Matsumoto and Jiro Kanno were waiting for her. The guard let her in; she gave him her name and he checked it against a list on a clipboard.

He told her to take the lift on the far right, which went straight to the penthouse, where Matsumoto Studios resided. The fast whoosh of the lift combined with the butterflies in her stomach made her flush. She was so nervous.

The door flashed open. The first thing she was greeted with was a life-size cutout of Tadao. What a thrill! His big shiny eyes gazed at Kiyoko as she brushed past him, murmuring in Japanese, "I'm sorry they killed you."

Drinking in every detail—from the pulsating, driving thrash metal piped through the speakers to the anime characters in Day-Glo colors lining the black walls of a long corridor, Kiyoko was so nervous and so amped, she was afraid she was going to faint dead away. She knew people who would give vast sums to be in her place. She took careful mental notes so she could tell the lads back in her online bulletin boards everything she could about the offices.

The corridor let out into a large square room lined with computers and electronics. There was a ton of equipment, and some of it looked out of date. A guitar, a tambourine, and a violin were grouped on a gunmetal gray workstation.

The floor was maroon tile, and there was an eight-foot-tall waterfall splashing into a pond shaped like a piece of *edamame*—a soybean—on the other side of the room.

"There you are," Matsumoto-san said to her, giving her a perfunctory bow. He turned and said over his shoulder, "Jiro-kun, Katsuda-san is here."

Jiro Kanno emerged from a closed door. He bobbed his head at her. Both men seemed preoccupied, and she wondered if the extra hour she had requested had been a problem. She wasn't about to ask them that, though. Because what if they said that it had been?

He and Jiro sat in overstuffed chairs across from a yellow leather couch. There was a coffee table between the chairs and the sofa, and Matsumoto-san invited her to sit on the couch.

"So. There are so many questions I want to ask you."

She licked her lips. "Your influences are . . . ah . . ." She was panicking. *I forgot to think up questions to ask them!*

Stop. You are Kiyoko! You think on your feet. Just do it.

"Your influences are Germanic," she said. "Wagner. You use the concept of the leitmotif."

They stared at her. "Yes, we do," Kanno-san said. "I'm astonished."

Music is my thing. This is my thing!

"I . . . I know this, and I tried to do the same thing in some music *I* wrote," she said. "May I show you?"

"Oh," Matsumoto frowned slightly. "I suppose."

Kiyoko extracted her laptop from her satchel. She looked around and said, "Um. Do you have a pair of external speakers that I might use?"

Matsumoto-san's eyelids flickered. "Not here," he said.

No speakers in a music studio? Kiyoko was freaked out all over again. Maybe she should have brought some speakers. Maybe . . .

. . . maybe her laptop wasn't coming on.

Did I forget to charge it? she wondered, panicking. With shaking hands, she rummaged around for the power cord.

She hadn't brought it.

She closed her eyes and took a deep breath. "I'm so sorry," she said in Japanese. "May I please borrow a power cord?"

Matsumoto frowned again. Then he got up and crossed to one of the computers lining the wall. He selected a power cord and brought it back to her, holding it out without a word.

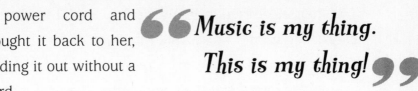

"Music is my thing. This is my thing!"

Her face was hot. She bowed her thanks and took the cord, plugging it into the wall and the outlet on the computer. The computer booted up.

Matsumoto-san sat back down. Jiro Kanno shifted his attention, resting his hands on his knees as he gazed down at the floor, preparing to listen.

Taking a deep breath, Kiyoko hit Play.

Her little playlist cycled through in less than five minutes. She was shocked that it was so short. Had she accidentally deleted some of her songs?

"Um," she said, searching. But no, that was it.

"So," she said, smiling her frozen smile again. "Did you like it?"

Matsumoto-san and Kanno-san exchanged looks. Kiyoko's forehead beaded up with sweat. She was freaking out.

"I picked out my best," she continued. "But I have others—"

"Katsuda-san," Matsumoto-san cut in. "I thought you wanted to interview us."

"I do," she said. "I was just hoping . . ."

Then the great Jiro Kanno, her complete and total idol, crossed his legs and arms and leaned back in his chair. He said, "I couldn't help but notice your last name. Katsuda is, of course, revered in many circles. I took the liberty of researching it, and I discovered that you are the daughter of Hideo Katsuda."

"Yes, I am," she said, wondering what he was going to say next. Ask her if her father could do him a favor? Maybe try to use the connection to get some money or meet a movie star or something?

"Well, on that subject, let me say this," Kanno-san said, looking at her levelly. "You're obviously a spoiled rich girl, who thinks nothing of wasting the time of very busy people in order to indulge her own whims and fantasies."

"No," she protested faintly. She thought she was going to faint.

He pointed at her laptop. "Nothing you played for us is remotely finished, is it? You cobbled something together at the last minute. Didn't you?"

"Sir, I have to work very hard at *Flirt*," she began.

He waved her off. "We have to work very hard as well. So we don't appreciate it when someone wastes our time like this."

Beside him, Shinichiro Matsumoto scowled like a dark thunder god.

Her cheeks stung exactly as if one of them had reached out and slapped her. She was so hurt, she couldn't speak. With trembling hands, she closed the laptop and replaced it in her bag. Then she silently got up and left the room. Neither Matsumoto-san nor Kanno-san said a single word to stop her.

Tears streamed down her cheeks as she stumbled back through the corridor.

⊚　　⊚　　⊚　　⊚

"Oh, God, Matteo," Kiyoko sobbed into the phone. "It was so humiliating!"

"They're jerks," Matteo said on the other end. "Power-tripping you to protect their territory. They'll probably steal your best work and—"

"You haven't been listening! There *was* no best work! It was a terrible botch. Oh, my God." She wept harder. "I was so distracted. There was the party, and . . . oh, forget it, I can't put the blame on anyone but myself."

"That's ridiculous," he insisted. "How can you be creative when you're living in a fishbowl? Maybe you should rent a studio of your own, get some equipment and—"

"And what?" she interrupted.

"Try again. Tell them you want another chance."

She shook her head, even though he couldn't see her. "There's no way. They booted me! They never want to speak to me again."

"I'm sorry, baby." His voice was gentle, soothing. "Hold on."

In a few seconds, a picture of his lips kissing the display arrived. She laughed weakly, wiping her eyes.

"You're so sweet," she said. She took a picture of herself kissing the screen and sent it to him.

She returned to the loft and found Mel and Alexa eagerly waiting for her. One look at her tear-streaked face told them all they needed to know. They hustled her into their room while she poured out the story of her total humiliation.

"Oh, Kiyoko, I'm so sorry," Mel said, giving her a hug. "We should have tried harder to help you."

"No." Kiyoko shook her head. "There was nothing for you to do. I needed to stay in here and get it done, and I didn't. They were right. I *am* nothing but a spoiled rich girl."

"No, you're very talented," Alexa asserted. "You're cutting-edge. They just didn't notice."

Kiyoko shook her head. "Everyone's been right about me. I'm a scatter-head. I start a million things, and I never finish anything. No wonder Ms. Bishop doesn't think I'm taking my internship seriously."

"What?" Mel cried. "She is just wrong!"

Kiyoko remembered that she hadn't told either of them about the conversation she had had with Emma. Now she described the entire hideous exchange, and they stared at her in dismay.

"All I've been doing is proving her right," Kiyoko said miserably.

"Then stop," Mel counseled. "You have that article to do on freeback, right? Didn't Liv mention a club while we were in the park this afternoon?"

"Yes, we're going tomorrow," Kiyoko said. "You

mates are going too, right?"

"Let's go tonight!" Alexa said. She snapped her fingers like castanets. "We'll have fun and investigate at the same time, *si*?"

Before Kiyoko could reply, Alexa took Kiyoko's hand and led her out of their room. "Let's wash your face and get all pretty and have a wonderful time. We're sixteen years old and we're in New York City. It is *not* the time for tears and gloom."

"Alexa's right," Mel asserted, following after them. "Tonight is the first night of the rest of our internship. Don't let all this negativity get you down."

Never in a million years had Kiyoko dreamed she could cheer up. But the girls' enthusiasm was catching. She was actually beginning to feel good.

"But it's bloody freeback," Kiyoko mock-grumped.

"In a bloody freeback *club*," Alexa retorted. She waggled her brows. *"Vamos a bailar!"*

"All right," Kiyoko consented grandly, and she actually smiled.

chapter nine

Clubbing! After totally going down in flames, Kiyoko couldn't believe she was heading to Café Endless, aka freeback central, to celebrate her self-destruction by partying down to terrifically bad music. Liv was happy to move the field trip up and serve as Kiyoko's guide. So there she was, laughing in a cab with her three mates, less than an hour after her complete annihilation. Maybe Matsumoto and Kanno had crushed her ego as completely as Godzilla had crushed Tokyo. But the girls were right. She had to have hope. After all, Godzilla reformed and became the friend of the Japanese people. Maybe someday she would get another chance to impress her idols.

The girls had glammed up for their night out—little black dresses, lots of body sparkle, high heels, the works. Kiyoko went backless and asked Alexa to help her apply a temporary tattoo of the kanji character for "warrior" between her shoulder blades. *Aiya!* She was invincible!

It was a hot New York night, and they were hot chickadees on the prowl for fun times . . . Even better,

Kiyoko had researched the club and had discovered that the famous writer Robert Varrdeman had planted his famous butt in one of the booths night after night, penning *Traumaland,* his work of poetic genius. As she knew it would, that thrilled Mel so thoroughly that the lad practically wet her pants.

"If he sat in this club, he probably went deaf," Kiyoko drawled as their cab pulled up outside a three-story brownstone covered in neon. A tall tree sparkled with twinkling lights. Overhead, a black awning flashed with a crawl that said *Café Endlessendlessendless . . .*

Through the cab window, the steady rhythm vibrated through Kiyoko's body—*dum-dum-dum-dum*. Next came the inevitable shift in tempo—ah there it was—*dum-dum-dum-dum-dum*.

That was it. *Dumb.* The total musical experience of freeback. She still thought it was idiotic, but it did beat weeping on the phone to Matteo.

"This club used to be a speakeasy," she informed them. "Those were clubs that served alcohol when it was illegal in the United States."

"A speakeasy," Alexa said, rolling the word on her tongue.

"That's easy for you to say," Kiyoko replied, and she and Alexa cracked up.

Kiyoko paid the cabbie, who took her wad of cash without even saying thank-you. New York.

It was only nine thirty, still unspeakably early for the

club scene, but there was already a queue halfway around the block. The crowd looked to be slightly older than the Four *Flirt* Musketeers, maybe early twenties. Everyone was extremely fashionable, sleek, and polished—Upper East Siders. They were definitely not the funky, edgy folk Kiyoko preferred. Not a musician or an artist in the bunch, she was willing to guess.

Artists made her think of Nick Lyric, which made her think of Matteo. She pulled out her Razr and texted him. *Doko ni?* which was a shortened version in Japanese of "Where are you?" She wanted to tell him she was regrouping.

> **But she had her mates. Mates were good.**

He didn't reply. It occurred to her that it *would* be rather nice to have a boyfriend who was actually present during her crises. But she had her mates. Mates were good.

Liv walked right up to the bouncer and flashed him her *Flirt* badge. The bouncer lifted the maroon velvet rope and gestured for Liv to enter, to the howls of indignation of those in the queue. Liv ducked underneath, gesturing to her mates.

The others sashayed behind her, striding past the propped-open entry door, and into a long, narrow corridor painted glow-in-the-dark green with the words *Café Endless* stenciled on the walls in black. There was another queue, this one much shorter. A thirtysomething guy in a black suit with a white shirt and bolo tie held court behind a podium with a green study lamp, which provided enough light for him to check IDs and accept the payments for the cover charge.

"The cover charge is twenty dollars?" Mel looked queasy. "We should have called ahead and told them we were with *Flirt.*"

"Well, we didn't," Kiyoko said. "It's all right, really."

"Yes, it would be triple that in London," Liv assured her.

"We're not in London," Mel said.

"No, we're in New York," Liv countered. "Which is nearly as expensive as London."

"London prices are crazy," Kiyoko said. "Have you priced steel-toed boots and fishnets on Oxford Street?" She crossed her eyes.

"Well, twenty dollars is crazy in any country," Mel huffed. Beside her, Alexa nodded vigorously.

"Seguro," she said. *"Totalmente loco."*

"Maybe we should skip it," Mel continued, and Alexa nodded. Kiyoko wanted to say to them, *Stop! You do this every time.*

"Easy, lads," Kiyoko said instead. "Let trained professionals handle this. *Please.*"

"I'll do it," Liv said. She transacted. Their IDs were checked—three passports and a California driver's license—then each of them was fitted with a purple plastic wristband that would join Kiyoko's collection at night's end.

Purple meant they were too young to drink. Green was the color of the over-twenty-ones. It would be a simple matter to chat someone up and get them to buy her whatever she wanted. *If she wanted.* She had invited Spider, but he had texted back:

SPIDER_K: FREEBACK? RU CRZY?!

Tonight she was in the mood for boilermakers.

After they were done with check-in, the four strutted into the world of Café Tasteless. Really, it was so out-of-date, it was almost stylishly retro—strobe lights flashing over gyrating bodies, neon bands striping the walls, glittering drink glasses containing twinkling plastic ice cubes, and loud bad music.

"Oh, yeah, this place has it goin' on," Kiyoko said sarcastically. Alexa seemed to be the only one who heard her. Sparkling as only Alexa could, she wriggled her hips and clicked her fingers, finding her chica-snappa groove thang while Kiyoko surveyed the landscape.

"Where did Varrdeman actually sit?" Mel yelled into Kiyoko's ear.

"It said the booth behind the DJ's booth," Kiyoko said, pointing across the terrifically crowded dance floor in the direction of the—

Of the—

Wow.

The DJ was totally, nonironically gorgeous. Brown

hair. Dark, lovely eyes in a face with a square jaw and a bit of bristle. Wearing a black scoop-neck, long-sleeve T-shirt that displayed shoulders and a chest of the gods. He was busily punching in some code—digital playlist, Kiyoko guessed.

A waitress walked up and handed him a Pellegrino in a green glass bottle. He smiled his thanks at the waitress with dimples on dimples on dimples.

"He cannot seriously love freeback," Kiyoko shouted in Liv's ear.

"He's Cody. A true master. His sets are brilliant," Liv replied. "He tells stories with the music. It's fantastic."

"Do you know him?" Kiyoko asked Liv.

She shook her head. "I've only been in here a couple of times. I wonder if my friends are here . . ." She looked around and pulled out her BlackBerry. "I'll check in with them."

Kiyoko's attention swerved back to the handsome DJ. Wearing a head mic, he was bobbing his head along to the music. He caught the shift in tempo perfectly and took another swig of Pellegrino.

Then he said into the mic, "That's a cover of 'Nights in White Satin' by the Moody Blues. She walked into the satiny night; she was a purple haze; she was the end of days."

"See? It's a story," Liv said. "He starts one at the beginning of every set and makes it up as he goes."

"Art meets freeback," Kiyoko said, cocking her head.

"That's a surprise."

"Oh, Kiyoko, he'll be a great interview," Mel enthused. She pointed. "The booth behind him is empty. I want to sit where Varrdeman sat."

"Then let's go," Kiyoko said, leading the way. She couldn't stop staring at the DJ—at Cody. But she was moving on. Being professional. She was here to do research, not to lose her head—or anything else—over a pretty face.

They slid into the booth, Liv first in her slinky dress. Alexa sat beside her. Mel took the inside right. Kiyoko plopped down as Liv grabbed the menu.

"Fancy a nibble?" Liv asked the group. At the loft, the others had devoured a dinner of salad and portobello mushroom open-faced sandwiches while Kiyoko had been off humiliating herself at Matsumoto's office.

A waiter glided over. "May I start you ladies off with something?"

"Yes," Kiyoko said decisively. "Tempura veggies, black bean nachos, mozzarella and tomatoes, and the marinated cucumbers and mushrooms." She smiled at the girls, who were staring back at her in surprise. "That's something for everyone, yes?"

"Quite," Liv said. Everyone else nodded enthusiastically.

"And a boilermaker," Kiyoko concluded, beaming at the waiter.

The waiter made a sad face and pointed to her bracelet. He said, "I'm sorry, but you're underage."

> **She crunched and munched to the background disaster that was freeback. Listening. Researching. It got no better with familiarity.**

"In America, I'm underage," Kiyoko corrected him. Then she grinned and said, "Make it a virgin boilermaker. Out of a diet cola."

"You got it," he said.

The others ordered similar nonalcoholic drinks.

The food arrived with a jillion little white plates, a clatter of forks, and the drinks. Kiyoko dove in, sampling some of everything, which was the way life should be. She crunched and munched to the background disaster that was freeback. Listening. Researching. It got no better with familiarity.

Then DJ Cody spoke into his mic again, "As she sat with friends, my heart wondered how it would begin. Would she build me a stairway to heaven?"

"Led Zeppelin," Kiyoko told the others. "'Stairway to Heaven.'"

"I think he's talking about *you*, Kiyoko," Mel said as she stabbed a mushroom with her fork. She chewed thoughtfully. "You walked in; you're sitting with friends."

"So are half the people in this place, lad," Kiyoko retorted. But she wondered if Mel had a point. That might be kind of cool.

Kiyoko tried to parse which song he was playing, because it *wasn't* a cover of "Stairway to Heaven." Maybe Cody could weave a sort of story between the stories, but not with the freeback singles he played.

"Lurker at three o'clock," Liv told Kiyoko.

"Excuse me, wanna dance?" asked a deep, Bronx voice as Kiyoko glanced to her right.

Kiyoko's potential partner was a tall, blond guy with a goatee—over—wearing black silk cargo pants—so over—and a gold chain around his neck—over when Kiyoko's own father was his age. There was also tobacco smoke on his breath, which completely made her want to vomit.

But he was still a dance partner, and she was too edgy to just sit and stew. So she said, "Okay," and got to her feet.

"Have fun!" Mel called after her.

Kiyoko glanced at her mates over her shoulder. They were all giggling and wiggling their fingers at her as if it was too funny that she was actually going to dance with the guy.

Together they inched through the packed crowd to the equally packed dance floor. It was difficult maneuvering; Kiyoko was briefly homesick for the sardine-can trains of Tokyo. *If this many people are dancing to freeback, maybe it's not as over as I thought*, she mused. *No. I'm right. I've read* Billboard. *No one is buying freeback albums anymore. These people are cultural dinosaurs. This club is their tar pit.*

Moving to the beat(s), Kiyoko's escort threaded his

way between all the dancers, seeming to need to reach a particular destination the way those adorable penguins in that movie had to tromp across the ice floes of the Antarctic before they could lay their eggs. As Kiyoko's good fortune would have it, his roosting spot just happened to be directly in front of the DJ's glass booth.

Oishii, Kiyoko thought, *tasty,* as she glanced at DJ Cody. She wanted to snap a picture and send it to Miko. It was a little past two A.M. in London. Miko was probably at some young aristo's swanky party.

Cody was staring right at her. He smiled sexily, raising one brow, and put his bottle to his lips. She grinned back.

Kiyoko's dance partner started going through his routine. He wasn't too bad. Clubbers usually either danced well, or they stuck to the booths and drank. Freeback gave one the advantage of a very clear beat. Not that Kiyoko needed one. She was a good dancer, if she did say so herself.

"So, you come here often?" dance guy said, breathing his stinking eau de Marlboros all over her.

"Never."

He nodded, smiling. She wondered if he had actually heard what she'd said.

The left side of Cody's mouth quirked upward, as if he knew that she was hating the music he played for a living. If that kept him smiling, Kiyoko was all for it. She worked on hating it some more.

She and the smoker danced for about six years; then the long, boring, pointless song segued into another long, boring, pointless song as Cody said into a microphone, "Lovely one, disdain. Moves to my freeback rhythm. Her eyes remain closed."

"Haiku," Kiyoko said aloud. She gave him a slow nod to show her appreciation; but at the same moment, a waitress handed him a piece of paper. It was probably a request. Had to be; there was some money attached to it. Looked to be a fiver.

> **His eyes were the color of dark chocolate.**

"That's enough for me," Kiyoko's dance partner announced at the conclusion of the song. He fanned himself and pantomimed smoking. "I'm going outside. Join me?"

"Go on ahead." She gave him a farewell wave.

Then she was dancing alone, which was actually preferable, and as she moved in a slow circle . . .

. . . *he* was watching her.

She was a combination of shy and show-offy as she made another circle. She wondered if he liked what he saw. *She* did.

It's okay to look, she reminded herself. *It's okay to flirt.*

After all, I do it all the time.

So the next time she came back around and he raised his Pellegrino bottle in salute, she smiled at him.

"I'm going to take a short break," Cody said into the mic. "Next set starts in fifteen. First up will be a special request to Kiko from the brats."

Kiyoko laughed and waved at her friends. Eli, Ben, and a guy and a girl she didn't recognize had crammed into the booth. Alexa blew Kiyoko a kiss. She elbowed Mel, and Mel waved. They had drinks with flashing ice cubes in them.

Kiyoko started to head toward them when the deep, honey voice of the DJ permeated her space.

"You're new," he said.

She turned and gave him a look. "I'm Kiyoko."

He held out his hand. "Cody Sammarkand."

They shook hands. His eyes were the color of dark chocolate.

"Are you from Uzbekistan?" There was a city called Samarkand in Uzbekistan.

She was getting an excellent education at her private school in Tokyo.

"Well, you know your geography."

She said, "I'm with *Flirt*. I'm doing a piece on freeback. Can I interview you?"

He put his hands in his pockets and rocked back on his heels. "Sure."

"Good." She brightened. "When?"

"Want to start now? I have a dressing room." He pointed to a door stenciled with the words *Employees Only*. "Nothing weird. Just peace and quiet."

"Fine," she said.

"Okay." He held up his Pellegrino. "Would you like something to drink?"

She nodded. "A boilermaker."

He cocked his head. "You're wearing a purple bracelet."

"I'm incognito." She wrinkled her nose. "It's a joke, lad. At this point, bottled water will be fine, thanks."

Cody gestured to a waitress, who hustled over and took his order for two soda waters with cranberry juice.

"Would you mind bringing them to my dressing room, Delores?" he asked her, covering both of her hands in one of his. "This nice lady is a reporter."

"Oh. Sure!" Delores looked excited and possibly also relieved. Kiyoko wondered if they were sweeties, and Delores was therefore reassuring herself that no one else had caught Cody's brown velvet eye.

Kiyoko bounded back to the booth to get her purse and say hi to Ben and Eli. Her mates introduced her quickly to the strangers—seemed they were friends of Liv's. The guy actually said, "Chahmed, I'm sure," like an aristo in a low-budget American movie, and Kiyoko wondered if he was having her on.

"Purse, please. I'm interviewing him," she told the lads. Mel turned to look for her straw cylinder, and Alexa gave her a thumbs-up. Liv smiled in a preening sort of way as if to say, *You see? I know what I'm about.*

Mel handed over the purse; Kiyoko unzipped it and

then she remembered that she still hadn't gotten new batteries for her tape recorder. No problem. She would improvise.

And she'd do a good job, too.

She went back to Cody. He led the way through the door and down a hall. The music was muffled—a distinct relief—and then he escorted her into a small room furnished with a black leather couch, two red chairs, a bulbous purple thing that looked like a CD player, and a water cooler.

"Please, sit," he invited her. "Did you bring your tape recorder?"

"No. First I take notes," she said breezily. "I tape the second interview."

"Oh?" His eyes crinkled. "So this is an ongoing process."

"Yes." She dimpled as she hauled out . . . she had no notebook.

He waited. She clasped her hands around her knees and said, "I take *mental* notes. Please spell your name."

He did so.

She launched.

"Why freeback?"

"It's the rage," he replied without hesitation. "People love it. The combination of the great lyrics and the shifting rhythms . . . it's unlike anything else."

"Hmm." She nodded thoughtfully. *How could anyone so handsome have so little taste?* If lack of taste he honestly had. Perhaps what was really going on was TV talk. He couldn't exactly tell her that he loathed freeback and that the disc jockey gig was so his poor mum could have a liver transplant, could he?

So what was she to do? Unless she could pry something loose from him, it was going to be a very boring interview.

"To be honest," she said, "I loathe the stuff. I think it's over, and I'm only doing this because my bosses are forcing me to."

He looked at her as if he were making some kind of decision. She mentally crossed her fingers, praying that he confess all to her, or at the very least, give her a dishy quote. Her brain began creating a Deep Content page for him . . . until she remembered that print was passé and she needed to think about the grid.

So . . . musical annotations! Samples of songs, overlaid with his voice, and the original songs, in the case of covers. She could hear it all very clearly. She smiled to herself. The grid was cool.

He said, "Freeback is one of the fundamental new sounds."

Ack. She rolled her eyes. "You don't really believe that. You're just saying that."

He held up a finger. "But here's one that's even newer."

He reached over the arm of his chair and picked up the CD player. The power light was already on; he pressed Play.

Something very different undulated from the

speakers. It was slow, sinuous, and dreamy. She heard definite orchestral strains that she knew very well.

"That's Jiro Kanno," she said.

"Ah. You know your anime," he said, shaking his head. "You're close, but it's not Jiro Kanno."

She stared at him. "You know who Jiro Kanno is?"

He held out his hands. "Only the most influential Japanese composer working today."

Oh, my God. She was completely blown out of the water. Who would have thought? Who would have known? A fellow disciple dwelled in a freeback club!

"What's your favorite piece by him?" she asked.

"Hands down, 'Tadao's Theme.'"

"That's my favorite, too." She felt warm. She felt dizzy. "This is not some cruel hoax, is it?" she asked anxiously.

He chuckled. "Listen."

She did. The music . . . *curled* around her earlobes. It was so there, it was almost as if it were touching her. Then the melody handed off to the beat, which was a steady four-four, while the melody slid like silk over her bare arms. Then the time signature changed to three-four—a waltz, but much more slowly and deliberately than the awkward rhythm shifts of traditional freeback.

It was the coolest thing she had ever heard.

She listened with her eyes closed. There was a knock on the door, and Cody rose to get it.

The song ended and she opened her eyes with a

sigh. When he returned, he was carrying two drinks in his hands, and a bottle of water was tucked under his arm. He set them down.

"Isn't that incredible?" he asked her as he sat back down in his chair.

"Yes." And what was even more incredible was that he felt that way. She was all a-tingle.

But she wouldn't let him know that, of course. "What do you call it, post-freeback?" she asked.

"No. It's manga psychedelic."

I love it! What a cool name! This is so cool! "How come I've never heard of it? I'm pretty jacked in."

He laughed. "It's street music. It came from the Harajuku scene."

"Oh?" She was intrigued that he knew about Harajuku. "Have you been?"

He nodded. *"Omoshiroi."*

She grinned at him. She liked him so much, she wanted to bite him. *Omoshiroi* meant "interesting" in Japanese. "Interesting" was a big compliment in Japanese. Harajuku on Sundays was always interesting. Harajuku was a section of Tokyo, and street bands thronged there to perform on Sundays, usually in heavily themed costumes. They would line the walkways, playing all kinds of music from rockabilly and doo-wop to thrash metal in precisely staged performances that would put many professionals to shame. There were several anime groups, including at least two that specialized in Jiro Kanno. They dressed up like

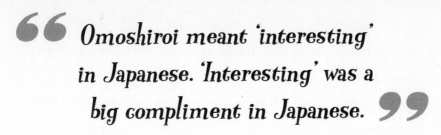

> ## " *Omoshiroi meant 'interesting'*
> *in Japanese. 'Interesting' was a*
> *big compliment in Japanese.* "

some of Matsumoto-san's most famous characters—Tadao, Jun Kobayashi, Sensei Kira, and the Flower Princess—and conducted sing-alongs with the crowds that gathered to watch them.

"Well, I think manga psychedelic is *omoshiroi*, but I think freeback is lame," Kiyoko informed him. "All it has going for it is the changing backbeat. Otherwise . . . *pfft.*"

"You're wrong," he told her.

"I'm not." She gestured to the CD. Her hands were almost shaking, she was so excited. This night was not all shot to hell after all! "Do you have more of that?"

He nodded. "I'll burn some for you."

"Arigato," she said, bowing.

"Domo," he replied, bowing back. "I have to go back in a few. How would you like to take a spin at DJing? For your research?"

"Love to!" she cried, clapping her hands.

"You're not big with the fear gene, are you?" he asked her.

She laughed. "Lad, I've done it before."

"You've had a varied career as a person," he said, sounding impressed.

"I'll shine," she promised him.

"Okay, let's go," he said. He took her hand and helped her up from her chair. Little tingles skittered up and down her arm.

They left the little break room and went back out into the club. Cody led her over to his station—which consisted of several towers of CDs and a simple computer system. He said, "I have a lot on digital, but not all of it. I program my playlists, but I can change them if I want. Here's how to input something."

He showed her how. They spent a good five minutes on it.

"And it's showtime in three," he told her. "You ready?"

"Of course!" Kiyoko informed him.

⊚　　⊚　　⊚　　⊚

And she did shine, just as she had promised. With her amalgamated lingo and her verve, she had the lads in Café Endless whirling and dancing. And as Cody explained to her, whirling and dancing was what it was all about, because it ensured people were having fun. And people who had fun stayed at the club, ordered drinks, food, and told their friends to meet them there.

Just like Liv, whose two aristo mates were joined by three more. Pretty soon, the Varrdeman booth was Club Liv.

"Here's one for England!" Kiyoko said into the mic.

All of Liv's friends hoisted their glasses.

"And all my mates!" Kiyoko cried.

More cheering from the entire booth.

"Let's hear it for freeback!" Kiyoko yelled.

Mel, Alexa, and Ben burst into hysterics. They pushed their way out of the booth and worked their way onto the dance floor, dancing all crazy-wild together as Kiyoko pumped up the volume.

"Easy, easy," Cody told her. "We have a decibel restriction." He was laughing and shaking his head. "I thought you hated this stuff."

> **And she did shine, just as she had promised.**

She made sure her mic was off and said, "I like what it's doing, that's for certain."

He gazed at her. "What's it doing, Kiyoko Katsuda?"

She caught her breath. He was so seriously handsome. And he smelled so good. But she had a *tomo-boyu*, and she really, truly adored him best. So she took a discreet step back—emotionally—and made her smile a little less welcoming.

"It's making people happy," she replied.

Then there was a big stir throughout the club. People turning, rising from their booths. It was a ripple effect, and Kiyoko looked in the direction everyone else was looking, highly intrigued.

And then she saw who had just walked in: short, sassy, dressed in a slashed-up very cool *thing* that might have been a dress but now was sort of a wrapper, and sandals that laced up to below her knees.

Kiyoko waved and said into her mic, "And one for Belle Holder!"

Beside her, Cody gasped and said, "Oh, my God, I can't believe it. Belle Holder's in the club?"

"Yeah. She's my new boss," Kiyoko told him.

Cody stared at her. The wonder on his face was . . . kewl.

"I could seriously love you," he said, and moved in to kiss her.

chapter ten

KIYOKO'S BLOG:

Kiyoko loves Matteo. As soon as I realized what was happening, I took a step away from Cody. The lovesick lad held out his arms as if to say, "Can you blame me?" and how could I? So I crossed my eyes at him and he laughed, and that was the end of all that nonsense!
MOOD: FLIRTATIOUS!
MUSIC: FREEBACK, BABY!

Surrounded by people, Belle watched Kiyoko's spin as a freeback DJ with a mixture of amusement and something else Kiyoko could not translate, all the while yakking with Mel, who kept glancing over at Kiyoko as if to say, "Isn't this cool? I can't believe how cool this is!"

Kiyoko herself was beyond jazzed. After the long, frustrating day she had had, her triumph was sweet. Standing so closely beside her that she could feel his body heat, Cody beamed first at her and then at Belle—and Kiyoko was totally flattered (but not surprised!) that Cody could actually tear his gaze away from one of the giants of popular culture to stare at little ol' her.

Kiyoko said to Cody, "I don't mean to offend you, but I am totally shocked to see my boss in here."

Cody chuckled. "Kiyoko, this is one of the trendiest clubs in Manhattan. Sure the decor sucks, but the most beautiful of the beautiful will show up here in a couple of hours."

"Wow." Kiyoko couldn't wait.

Then Mel gave Kiyoko a wave and pantomimed pointing to a watch. *And it was eleven fifty-six!*

"Oh, my God!" Kiyoko shouted into the mic. Then she covered her mouth and silently said to Cody, *Sorry. Must go! Now!*

She tore off the mic, handing it to him.

"Wait, Cinderella!" he called after her.

She dashed out of the glass cubicle toward Mel and Belle at the next booth over from the Varrdeman booth. Liv and Alexa were draped over the back of the booth, heads craned toward Belle and Mel. Belle was hunkered over her cell—probably so she could be heard—with Melanie bent over beside her. Spotting Kiyoko, Mel gave Kiyoko a thumbs-up.

When Kiyoko reached them, Mel said, "I think it's okay. Belle told Emma we're with her. Emma said we should have called earlier, but this isn't going to count against us."

She looked a little worried. "I think."

"Glad to see you checked the place out," Belle said. "Good initiative. I told Irma you'd be back in about half an hour, so we should go."

"Emma," Kiyoko corrected her. "Thank you." Her nerves were jangled.

"So go say good night to the hunk-throb," Belle told her, grinning.

Kiyoko hesitated. She said, "I'm sure he would love to meet you. Would you mind?"

Belle smiled like an indulgent parent. "Sure." She looked around at everyone glommed around them and said, "Give me some space, people!"

A few gave ground, but not many, so Belle and her parade swarmed around the dancers like cicadas and reunited at the DJ booth. Then Kiyoko led the way into the glassed-off cubicle.

Cody said into the mic, "I smolder; she brings Belle Holder!"

The song that had been playing melted into a cover of "Fire" by Bruce Springsteen.

Cody took off his mic and held out his hand as Kiyoko said, "Belle, this is Cody Sammarkand. He's not from Uzbekistan."

"Hey." Belle shook his head. "I've heard about you. You are the freeback *man*."

Kiyoko could have knocked him over with a feather. "Thank you. And you are . . . Belle Holder," he said, agog.

"I am," she agreed. She gestured to his setup. "Phat."

"Thanks." He licked his lips. Kiyoko could see how nervous he was. "It's such an honor to meet you."

"Whatever." She shrugged. "Once you've been me for as long as I have, it's not that big a deal." She laughed at her own joke. Kiyoko and Cody laughed, too. She gestured to Kiyoko. "She's a pretty good DJ, wouldn't you say?"

"Yeah." He grinned at Kiyoko. "Who knew, given how much she hates—"

"Burn me some manga psychedelic."

"Crowds," Kiyoko said quickly. "I hate crowds so much!"

Cody looked a little confused but went along with her obvious need to conceal, saying, "Right. She can't stand the crowds."

"Listen, she's got to write this article for me, so I'm thinking, how about she guest DJs for a few nights?" Belle asked him.

Cody brightened. "Sick!" Then he hesitated. "But it's not up to me. I mean, it's totally good with me, but she'll have to ask the manager."

"I'll go do that," Belle said.

She turned on her heel and left the two alone. Cody reached for Kiyoko's hand. He said, "I can't believe I have actually met Belle Holder. What can I do to thank you?"

"Burn me some manga psychedelic," she replied.

"You got it." Cody paused.

She crossed her eyes again, and said, "Attention, attention. I have a boyfriend."

Cody's smile went a little flat. But it didn't disappear. He said, "Oh. Where is he?"

"California."

Cody's smile hit refresh.

☙   ☙   ☙   ☙

They limo'ed back to the loft. Emma, Nick, Gen, and Charlotte were waiting to meet Belle. As a former photographer for *Flirt*, Emma had met more than her share of celebrities, so she was her warm *Gilmore*-mom self without any frills. Nick was a lot more enthusiastic—"I always read your reviews before I buy anything," he told her. Gen and Charlotte were over the moon, seriously.

As everyone lounged in the sunken living room, drinking tea and winding down, Belle said to Emma, "I'm going to take Kiyoko off your hands for the next few nights, if that's all right with you."

Emma said, "The interns have a curfew."

"I'll need her until one tomorrow night. Then we can get her home by midnight on Sunday and Monday, how's that?"

Emma hesitated.

"Oh, please, dear lady," Kiyoko begged. "It's for my piece for the mag. I have got to do a good job."

"She'll go straight to the club and straight back," Belle assured her. "No side trips, no weirdness."

"Oh, let her," Mel urged Emma.

"You can call my parents for permission if you like," Kiyoko said. She'd get them to say yes even if they didn't want to.

That decided Emma. "All right. If the Katsudas say yes, and as long as she has adult supervision," Emma said.

Kiyoko and her mates gave a cheer. Gen, not so much. Charlotte merely smiled.

Belle said, "Great. Let's set up our battle plan." She turned to Alexa and wrinkled her nose. "You don't mind if I use your room for a confab?"

"Por favor," Alexa said generously.

"Thanks," Belle told her, sailing into their room with Kiyoko in tow.

Belle shut the door, "Okay. If your parents say it's all right, you'll guest DJ at Café Endless for the next four nights. You're going to record your thoughts and sample your sets." She gestured to Kiyoko's purse. "Take your recorder with you."

Kiyoko frowned. "Don't worry. I'm all about the memory these days." Then she realized Belle didn't know the whole sad story. She wasn't certain she would ever tell her about it, either.

Sunday.

Night number two of her four nights, and Kiyoko already had a fan club. As soon as she showed up at nine P.M., the bouncer waved her in, the cover-charge guy said hi, and Cody greeted her with a soft, warm kiss. It was a friendly kiss. So Kiyoko told herself.

Then they "suited up" in the booth, and Kiyoko recorded herself:

> KIYOKO: I still think freeback is lame. I don't get why all these people like it. What I like is playing music for them and seeing their reactions. That's the effect music has on me. Sweet!

During their breaks, she and Cody played around with manga psychedelic. Kiyoko brought her laptop and they composed little songs that had Kiyoko dancing around the room.

"I wish I had known about this stuff when I tried to impress Kanno-san," she confided in him, after she had told him about her humiliating "audition." "I think he would love this."

"Wouldn't he have heard of it?" Cody asked. "I mean, I've heard of it, and I wasn't in Japan for very long."

She thought about that for a moment. And then she realized that it wasn't so much that Jiro Kanno would love manga psychedelic. It was that *she* did. She loved it so much, she was writing pretty cool manga psychedelic music.

"Cody! I've totally, truly found my *thing*!" she cried. "I've found something I can really focus on! It's not just music. It's *my* music! What I like. What I'm drawn to."

Overjoyed, she threw her arms around him. "This is brill!" She popped a kiss on his cheek and whirled away. "It's fantastic! My thing!" She threw open her arms and threw back her head. "Oh, if only I could play these bits for them."

"Maybe you can," he ventured. "Maybe you could contact them and ask for another chance."

She shook her head. "I totally messed up my shot with them. I'm PNG with that lot—*persona non grata*. That chance will never come again." She stirred. "But let's not let that stop us from making beautiful music."

He regarded her fondly. "You're something else, you know that, don't you?" He keyed in some notes. Fabulous riffs and chords of manga psychedelic poured back out. "I want to resume work on my documentary about Harajuku. I'll be going back to school in September. U of Connecticut," he added for her benefit.

"Oh, I could totally help you," Kiyoko said. "I'm leaving, but we could send files back and forth when I get back to Tokyo."

"Then let me help you in return," he offered. "Tell me what Matsumoto and Kanno are looking for. Maybe we can make them some cues in manga psychedelic. We could even e-mail them some. Speaking of which." He wrote down his e-mail and his cell phone number. "Call me when you have some downtime. Make some time in your workday. Make it a priority."

Prioritizing. What a concept.

"So, like, how do you organize yourself?" Kiyoko asked Liv the next morning. They were doing a Starbucks confab. Liv was Top Diva when it came to the administrative side of life. Truth be told, it was a trifle off-putting to go to Liv for advice, so Kiyoko passive-aggressively slurped her latte just to needle the Queen of All Manners. But Kiyoko was **"Prioritizing. What a concept."** determined to pull herself out of the rut of OOCAO—Out of Control and Overloaded—she seemed to constantly fall into, and Liv Bourne-Cecil was the antithesis of all that was chaos in action.

It was Monday, the first day of their last week at *Flirt*. Alexa was on an early-morning photo shoot with Lynn. Mel was in early to proof something for Bishop. Kiyoko was due to DJ tonight. Everything was so intense. Everything demanded her full attention.

"Lists," Liv said. "You absolutely have to have lists. I learned by watching my mother. She breaks everything down into steps and substeps. She sits down and figures out exactly what she needs to do to accomplish each thing. Then she delegates as much of it as she can. Once she does that, she moves on." Liv snapped her fingers for emphasis.

"That sounds like a lot of work," Kiyoko said, sipping the hot coffee.

"It's a lot of work upfront. But once she has it organized, she can move on. It's not like when you suddenly realize the batteries in your tape recorder have worn down or you show up somewhere without any money," Liv observed. "She's planned for just about any contingency. She told me it took years of practice. She's incredibly disciplined."

Kiyoko was taking mental notes. "I always feel like I'm running to catch up," she admitted. "Like I'm already behind when I wake up. And when I'm at school . . ." She rolled her eyes. "Forget it! All those assignments . . ."

> **Kiyoko was determined to pull herself out of the rut of OOCAO— Out of Control and Overloaded—she seemed to constantly fall into.**

"Well, let's work out a list for you right now," Liv offered. "What are your priorities?"

"Keep Trey happy, work on my piece for Belle, DJ, and work on my manga psychedelic with Cody," she said.

Liv thought a moment. "Is that the right order?"

Kiyoko was confused. "What do you mean?"

"Is keeping Trey happy really your number-one priority? He's moving on, isn't he?"

Kiyoko's lips parted. Then she said, "You're right. My piece for Belle is more important."

"And the DJ part?" Liv pressed.

Kiyoko took another thoughtful sip. "Well, it's important to me so I can do the piece and work on my manga psychedelic." She grinned. "I need Cody for that, and he's at the club."

Liv smiled faintly. "You like him."

Kiyoko batted her arm. "Not *like* like, you pudding head."

Liv took a small, dainty sip of coffee. "Moving on," she said delicately. "Which is more important, your piece for Belle or your manga psychedelic compositions?"

"Blimey," Kiyoko said. "I think my manga psychedelic is more important than my piece. Liv, it's just so *me*. It's my thing."

"Truth? I could never make that choice," Liv said. She sounded impressed. "I'm about fulfilling the requirements." When Kiyoko looked worried, she added, "This is *your* list of priorities, Kiyoko, not mine. It's what's most important to *you.*" She cocked her head. "Why do you want to jeopardize your piece to work on it? What's the hurry?"

Kiyoko grimaced. "Okay, call me daft, but I've got this fantasy where I get it to Matsumoto and Kanno, and they love it."

Liv leaned forward. "Why daft? If there's one thing we've learned at *Flirt*, it's to dream big, isn't it? The people who work there didn't get their jobs based on their timidity. They take risks. They go after what they want. You made a mistake first time out with them, but you're not dead, you know."

"Wow." Kiyoko's eyes bulged. "I totally misjudged you, Liv. You're not a stuck-up, uptight, arrogant aristo snob after all."

"And you're not a scatterbrained, self-indulgent, theatrical lunatic," Liv returned sweetly.

"One could say we've grown this summer," Kiyoko ventured.

They clinked their coffee cups, raised them in the air, and drank deeply.

KIYOKO'S BLOG:

(MY LIST)
AS SOON AS I GET TO WORK . . .
1. CHECK ALL MESSAGES & MAKE
BELLE'S LIST.
2. TELL BELLE I HAVE ENOUGH MATERIAL

FOR PIECE.

3. HAVE LUNCH W/CODY & WORK ON MANGA PSYCHEDELIC.

4. WORK ON PIECE INSTEAD OF DJING.

But the best-laid plans . . .

"I want to talk about your piece today at lunch," Belle told Kiyoko. So Kiyoko called Cody to cancel. She realized she had an amazing life, considering that she was actually having another meal with Belle Holder, and she was bummed out about it.

They went to a cool place in the Village called La Bastide, and Belle said, "Tonight I want you to interview some of the club people about the direction they think freeback is taking. Its evolution."

Belle's phone went off. Then so did Kiyoko's.

"Hola!" It was Matteo!

"Tomo-boyu!" she cried. "How are you? What are you doing?"

"Thinking about you," he said.

"That can't be bad. This connection is excellent."

"Yes, it is." He chuckled.

"I'm at lunch with my boss," she ventured.

"Got it. Later, Ki."

"Okay, ciao-ciao."

She and Belle hung up simultaneously. Belle chuckled and said, "Okay, about your piece. Let's make a cut of it after lunch. You can use a couple of the sound bites you get tonight at the back end."

Wow. "Okay," Kiyoko said excitedly.

And they did. Belle ordered her to put the voice-mail system on and to ignore all calls. She said, "I *would* work on this with you tonight, but I'm meeting Jay Goldstein for drinks. You know who he is, right?"

Kiyoko caught her breath. "*Rolling Stone.* Big shot."

Belle grinned. "We call them senior editors. I want him to listen to your piece. I think you might have something unique here, Kiyoko."

"Wow. Thank you," Kiyoko said, not quite able to believe her ears. "Serious?"

Belle shrugged. "Who loves you, baby?"

They spent the entire afternoon working on it, repeatedly running it through a digital editing program, sweetening the sound. Belle cut and recut it, showing Kiyoko how to start with a thesis sentence, then back it up. They went over it for hours, tightening it up, finding a core theme that was quite a shocker:

KIYOKO: Freeback takes old rock classics and repackages them in a distinctive beat, and new listeners are buying these new tracks by the hundreds of thousands of copies.

No one's buying freeback CDs. That's because the hippest listeners aren't BUYING CDs. They're downloading their music from online sources. Artists are beginning to realize this. The old system, where artists hoped to be signed to a major label in order to get distributed, is dying. Now all that artists need is a good website and links to the major e-stores. And lucky older artists who are getting the freeback treatment are being rediscovered by these youthful consumers. Check it out . . .

That was followed by a varied sampling of Kiyoko's playlist and quotes from different people she had talked to at the club.

"It's tight, it's fun, it's cool," Belle told her, burning a CD. "I'll let Jay listen to it." She patted Kiyoko on the shoulders. "Get some good quotes tonight, okay?"

"Thank you." Kiyoko was so incredibly jazzed. Wait until she told everyone she had ever met!

"Okay, I'm out of here for the day," Belle said.

Kiyoko was a little taken aback. It was only three thirty. Belle hadn't done anything all day except help her with her piece.

"What do you want me to do with the rest of *my* day?" she asked Belle.

Belle reached up and tousled Kiyoko's hair. "Take off," she said. "You've worked hard all day. You're DJing tonight." As Kiyoko began to protest, she said, "Consider it a gift from me."

"Okay," Kiyoko said, still unsure if it was all right.

> **She looked like a hundred other Tokyo anime fangirls. They would never think she had changed her ways if she showed up looking like this.**

But she remembered her list of priorities.

As she dashed back to her desk to snag her purse, she realized her Razr was summoning her, with a download of a manga psychedelic cue she and Cody had composed.

"Hi," she began, but Cody interrupted her.

"Kiyoko? Did she tell you?" He sounded very weird.

"Is something wrong?"

"Kiyoko. Belle called Matsumoto and Kanno. Did you tell her what happened?"

She was dizzy. "What? What are you saying?"

"Somehow she found out about our manga psychedelic project and about you going there, and she called them. And they called me because they couldn't get a hold of you."

"They called?"

"They're still in town. They said we can come by any time before five."

"Oh, my God! Belle never said a word to me!"

"Maybe in case it didn't work out," Cody said.

"I don't know! But . . . Cody! This is our shot!" She ran her hand through her hair, laughing and terrified.

"I'll get out of here right now."

"Meet me ASAP. In front of their offices."

"On it," she assured him.

Slinging her straw purse over her shoulder, she trotted down the corridor of silver and glass toward the main lift.

"Oh, Kiyoko." It was Trey, walking toward her. "I need you to look over some video grabs and—"

Kiyoko took a deep breath. This was her boss, or her boss's boss . . . this was *Trey*. And she was going to . . .

. . . prioritize.

She exhaled, licked her lips, and said, "I'm sorry, Trey. But I'm on an errand. I'll get it for you . . . tomorrow. I'm very sorry!"

She sailed past him.

"What?" he called after her.

She did not turn back.

Steady, lad, steady, she told herself.

☺   ☺   ☺   ☺

Cody was at the curb, dressed in some DJ clothes—black on black, his hair spiked, carrying a small black leather briefcase. Kiyoko looked down at herself—she had on a baggy silk dress in a patchwork design, a pair of black calf-length leggings, and combat boots. She looked like a hundred other Tokyo anime fangirls. They would never think she had changed her ways if she showed up looking like this.

"I need different clothes," she insisted.

"Kiyoko, it's after four," Cody said. "They're only there until five. We have to go up there *now.*"

"Okay. Moment of weakness over." She grimaced. "This is my fate, Cody. Just to think. None of this would have happened if I had not been robbed by a guy who was *not* a famous Bulgarian!"

Cody gazed at her fondly.

"You fascinate me," he told her.

"You're *omoshiroi* as well," she replied.

Together they entered the building.

chapter eleven

They were waiting, Shinichiro Matsumoto and Jiro Kanno, the giants of the anime world.

But they were not smiling.

Kiyoko had the distinct impression that they were only going through the motions of inviting her back in order to appease Belle. She marveled at being that important. And also that kind.

"Good evening, gentlemen," Kiyoko said, bowing very low. "This is my partner, Cody Sammarkand."

"*Hajimemashite,*" Cody said flawlessly. *How do you do?*

That perked them up. They both bowed and introduced themselves in Japanese. Cody responded.

Matsumoto-san buzzed Hayeda-san and said, "Bring tea." Then he looked expectantly at Kiyoko. "Did you bring your own equipment?"

"Yes, sir," she said, swallowing hard and glancing over at Cody. He nodded, hefting the satchel. He popped it open and drew out Kiyoko's laptop and two small high-end speakers.

" It rose, crescendoed, dipped, floated. It was like a living thing. "

"Please, gentlemen, sit down and enjoy," Cody said.

Matsumoto-san took a place on the couch. Kanno-san sat in a chair.

Cody put the laptop on the coffee table and unraveled cables to the two speakers, placing them halfway across the room.

Kiyoko was a mess. But she kept a big smile plastered on her face.

Cody looked at her and inclined his head.

She pressed the keyboard to execute their music program, and when Cody came over to her and took her hand, she knew it was not a flirtatious gesture. It was for mutual moral support. His hand was just as clammy as hers.

The music undulated across the room. It filled the bubbles in the waterfall. It caressed Kiyoko's face.

She nearly wept. *Did we actually do this?*

It rose, crescendoed, dipped, floated. It was like a living thing.

It unfolded and danced.

Cody squeezed her hand. She squeezed back. She saw in his eyes that he knew they had done something amazing.

Then it was over, and silence filled the room.

Kiyoko heard her heart beat.

Then Kanno-san said softly, "Again, please."

Oh. My. Nondenominational. God.

　　　◎　　　◎　　　◎　　　◎

It was nearly nine o'clock.

Cody and Kiyoko were late for their DJ gig at Café Endless.

And Matsumoto-san and Kanno-san had missed their plane back to Tokyo.

They had uploaded Cody and Kiyoko's cues onto their own system and played them as they ran some rough animations. Over the last four hours, Cody and Matsumoto-san developed a story line for a potential new TV series. It would be called *Harajuku Angels*, about three groups of kids who performed in Harajuku on Sundays and joined forces to save the world from demons. There would be a freeback band, a heavy-metal band, and a manga psychedelic band.

If they got financing, they would hire Cody full-time to work on it. But for now, they would give him a development job. He would have to take a leave of absence from school and relocate to Tokyo for at least three months.

"We'll take care of that," Matsumoto-san had said with a wave of his hand.

As for Kiyoko, they were purchasing the rights from

her and Cody for their musical cues, with the option to buy more. Kanno would orchestrate them into a unified sound. Both Kiyoko and Cody would have credits in the film.

"For now, please trust us with a handshake," Matsumoto-san said to Kiyoko in Japanese. She had replied by bowing deeply.

At ten, Cody got a call from the club, demanding to know where he was. He said to Kiyoko, "I should at least show. I'll have to give my notice."

With more bows, Matsumoto-san and Kanno-san put them in a cab. As the door slammed shut and they took off for the freeback club, Cody leaned over and tried to kiss Kiyoko again.

As before, she turned her cheek and moved away.

Her cell phone rang. It was Belle.

"He loves it," she told Kiyoko. "Goldstein. Says if *Flirt* doesn't want it, he'll run it in this special Podcast they're going to do."

"What?" Could lightning strike twice?

"Yeah. I'll tell you more about it tomorrow. Getting those quotes?"

"Belle, thank you," she said. "Matsumoto and Kanno loved our work. How did you find out about it?"

Belle guffawed. "Kiyoko, I *am* a journalist."

"But . . ."

"Does it matter? We'll talk about that later. Tell me what they said."

She did. Belle listened.

"You guys are going to need representation," she said. "A manager. Want me to hook you up?"

"Why are you doing this?" Kiyoko asked her.

"You're my intern," Belle said.

ⓖ   ⓖ   ⓖ   ⓖ

The club was jumping. Cody got out first, and Kiyoko bounded out after him. They ducked under the rope as the bouncer held it up. The guy looked at Cody and shook his head.

"Man, are you in trouble," he said.

"It's cool," Cody said.

"No, I'm serious," the bouncer cut in. Then his attention was diverted by some kid trying to rush the line. "Hey! No one comes in unless I say so!"

Kiyoko and Cody hurried inside, past the cover-charge station, where the guy in the bolo tie waved a hand saying, "Cody!"

Cody waved back.

The strobes and the sounds and the throngs were a shock after the intense but relatively tranquil hours with Matsumoto and Kanno. Cody said to Kiyoko, "I'd better find Bob." Bob was the manager, Cody's boss and the man who had approved Kiyoko's guest stint as DJ.

But at that moment, the tall, beefy manager stomped up to them and shouted at Kiyoko, "Where have you two been?"

Then she looked past him.

Her mouth dropped open. *"Matteo?"*

It was her *tomo-boyu!* In the deeply tanned, sun-streaked, green-eyed flesh.

She ran to him. But the arms of Kiyoko's fortune-cookie man were crossed over his chest. His excruciatingly handsome face was pressed into a suspicious scowl as he looked from Cody to Kiyoko and back again.

Sounding hurt, Matteo said, "Surprise."

"Oh! Your birthday surprise was my surprise!" Kiyoko cried, throwing her arms around him. She raised on tiptoe to kiss him. "Thank you!"

"California," Cody said. "Nice to meet you." He didn't sound the least bit sincere.

"Cody's my partner, Matteo," she explained. "My business partner. We just sold some music, Matteo! To Matsumoto and Kanno!" She kissed him again, yanking on his hands and dancing from side to side. "Cody's got a job with them, and they're going to see us in Tokyo!"

"Us?"

"Look," Cody said, "it's not what you think . . ." He trailed off and looked questioningly at Kiyoko, as if to say, *Is it?*

Kiyoko kept hold of Matteo.

Cody said, "Why don't I catch you later?"

"Okay. Come on," she said to Matteo, shepherding him down the main corridor. "How did you find me?"

"I called the loft," he said, as if that were obvious.

> **She ran to him. But the arms of Kiyoko's fortune-cookie man were crossed over his chest.**

"They told me you were working here. Except, you weren't. No one knew where you were. Emma Lyric is about to call the cops."

"Oh, my God." Kiyoko fished inside her purse and pulled out her Razr. She demon-dialed Emma.

"Kiyoko?" Emma said as she picked up.

"I-I'm sorry," Kiyoko began. "I got held up. I'm fine."

"I want you to come back to the loft. Now," Emma said angrily.

"All right." She disconnected. Putting her Razr back in her purse, she said to Matteo, "Where are you staying?" Then she rushed on. "Oh, Matteo, please don't be angry with me. I haven't seen you all summer. I missed you."

He warmed a little. He said, "Hey, Ki. I shouldn't be so childish. It was a long flight. Kind of a letdown that you weren't home, you know? And then they called the club, and they said you hadn't shown. I got really scared. And then you just waltzed on in with that *guy*."

"We sold our work to them," she said, tugging on his arm. "They're hiring Cody! We're going to get a manager. Isn't that brill?"

He smiled. "Totally." He leaned over and kissed her. "Let's get a cab. I'm staying with a friend of my aunt's."

"Oh, you are so dear," she said. "You went to all this trouble for me."

"I did." He kissed her. She kissed him back.

Sweet.

☙   ☙   ☙   ☙

They got caught up in the cab. He accompanied her to the loft, introducing himself to Emma and the other girls. Gen gave him the eye, and Mel was especially sweet. Kiyoko realized that she had scared everybody. It would have been very easy to call and let them know where she was.

When she told them what had happened, everyone was thrilled for her . . . and Cody.

"Isn't she great?" Alexa asked Matteo. "A genius!"

"Yes." Matteo gazed down at her. "A genius."

He kissed her softly, then took the lift back down to the street. Kiyoko stood on the fire escape, watching him cross the street, and she had a strange, heavy sensation around her heart.

It's because I'm so jacked up, she told herself.

And she knew that was true, because she couldn't sleep all night.

☙   ☙   ☙   ☙

First thing, bright and early, Bishop sent for her.

Bishop was seated behind her desk like the evil Dowager Empress Noriko in *Spirit Team Rocket Patrol*. "You gave your work to a competitor," she said.

"No." Kiyoko sat up straight. "I didn't."

"Jay Goldstein and I play poker together. You were developing a piece for *Flirt* and you showed it to him before you showed it to me."

"Oh." She hadn't understood that that was a problem. She didn't know what to do. She didn't want Belle to get in trouble. But Belle had offered to take it to Jay Goldstein.

She said, "I didn't know it would cause a problem."

"Oh, come now," Bishop scoffed.

"I didn't. I'm only sixteen years old. And you should give me the benefit of the doubt," she said, flaring. She had just sold music to Jiro Kanno. She didn't scare as easily as she once did.

Bishop's eyes widened, then narrowed; she said, "You have stolen from this magazine."

"What?"

"Your time was our time. And you played around and worked on other things . . ."

"Okay." Kiyoko tried to keep her voice even, but it did shake a little. She got slowly to her feet. Her mind was working overtime. Her impulse was to laugh and be charming, make a little joke to defrost the frozen dragon lady before her. But Kiyoko was at a loss. Ms. Bishop had a point. Kiyoko hadn't always given *Flirt* her best. In fact,

> **"Kiyoko nearly dissolved into a puddle. She sensed that something had changed between Bishop and herself. She wasn't sure what."**

she never had.

"You're right," Kiyoko said simply. "I owe you. And I'm sorry."

They looked at each other. Kiyoko started to freak out, and then she remembered that she had a life—and a career—beyond these four walls. But she had defined that life here, begun her career here.

Ms. Bishop grinned—briefly. She leaned back in her chair and gestured for Kiyoko to sit in hers.

Kiyoko blinked, and sat.

"My first job, I worked for a design house in Paris," Ms. Bishop began.

"That would be Micheline," Kiyoko filled in.

Ms. Bishop inclined her head. "Micheline. I was accused of spying for a rival designer. I found out I was fired when they changed the locks . . . and didn't give me a new key. I was nearly arrested." That strange smile of hers flashed across her collagen-loving lips and high cheekbones. "That's not in my official biography, is it?"

"No," Kiyoko said, shocked, and not sure where this was going.

"Some of us take big risks," Ms. Bishop said. "Sometimes that's what it takes. You're an artist, Kiyoko. You're a gunslinger. I was like that, too. But now . . . a lot of what I do, I do to manage my organization. So *Flirt* can not only survive but thrive. It's pressure of another sort. Risks that are different. It would be very bad for business if I got arrested."

Kiyoko took that in.

"Tell me exactly what's so good about your piece. Why Jay liked it so much."

Kiyoko nearly dissolved into a puddle. She sensed that something had changed between Bishop and herself. She wasn't sure what. But she seized the moment.

"It's meant to be heard," she said eagerly. "That's why it's so perfect for the online network. Mr. Goldstein said he wanted it for a Podcast."

Bishop nodded. "Why do you think Ms. Holder showed it to him?"

At a loss, Kiyoko shook her head.

"I mean, consider it. I would have been well within my rights to fire her."

"She . . . she thought it was good." That didn't sound right, but Kiyoko didn't know how else to put it.

"And so . . . ?" Bishop led her.

Kiyoko swallowed. "I'm sorry. I don't know."

"It's true that when you work for someone, they expect your loyalty. They expect you to work for them. But here at *Flirt,* we look for spectacular people. People who challenge and push themselves. We invest in their eccentricities and pursuits, because that's what makes them unique.

"We have had you interns shadow individuals who are not replaceable. If we lost Trey, we wouldn't look for someone like him. We'd look for someone entirely different."

Kiyoko nervously licked her lips.

"Belle Holder is a remarkable woman, and you are lucky beyond words to have ended up with her just before your tenure here came to an end. I hope you realize what extraordinary lengths she went to on your behalf."

Kiyoko wrinkled her nose. "She made me write about freeback."

"A good journalist can write about any subject," Ms. Bishop insisted.

"I'm not a journalist," Kiyoko said. "I know that now."

"What are you, then?" Ms. Bishop asked her.

"I'm Kiyoko," Kiyoko told her proudly.

"Well, you're also my proof that this internship program is well worth all the headaches associated with it." A smile flickered across her face. "And there are a considerable number of those."

Many of which I caused, Kiyoko translated.

"But that's what I'm trying to explain to you," Bishop went on. "Ms. Holder was trying to help you find your individuality. Nurture your inner maverick. Be someone I can't replace."

Kiyoko was deeply moved. She tried hard to say something profound in return. But to her horror, she burst into tears and said in a rush, "I'm going to miss this whole daft chaotic asylum!"

They both looked a little shocked.

"You'll be back," the legend told her. "If you want."

☙   ☙   ☙   ☙

Kiyoko wobbled out of Ms. Bishop's office two minutes later. Her adrenaline rush was still coursing through her. That, and the wonderment at what had happened in Ms. Bishop's office. What the grande dame of fashion had said to her. The regard she held for Kiyoko. It was the last thing she had expected. And the best.

Then she walked into Entertainment, to find Belle in Trey's office, calmly unpacking a box of books. She was wearing a gauzy black dress and a pair of sandals—an outfit Kiyoko would never have imagined her wearing.

Trey's office was bare except for Trey's desk. Kiyoko raised her eyes questioningly, feeling a sharp pang. He hadn't said good-bye. She hadn't even realized he had moved to a different office.

Belle cocked her head and said, "Change is good, kid."

"Ms. Bishop was kind of mad at you," Kiyoko said. "At first."

Belle snorted. "Won't be the last time."

Kiyoko was fascinated. "Aren't you afraid she'll fire you someday? That you'll go too far?"

"And if she does?"

"Oh."

"Kiyoko, there's worse things that getting fired. There's not living. Not taking the risk. It's not worrying about getting fired. It's not getting fired *up*. Does that compute, Japanese girl?"

"Yes. It computes."

"You did it, girl. You got fired up." Belle tousled Kiyoko's hair.

"I hate it when you do that," Kiyoko blurted. Then she covered her mouth with her hands, unable to believe she'd spoken her thoughts aloud.

Belle guffawed. "Good for you. That's what I'm talking about, Kiyoko. People with an attitude like that—and I'm not talking *attitude* attitude—they can't be fired. Because their career is finding venues to express their individuality. And people sometimes pay them handsomely to do it."

"That's kind of what Ms. Bishop told me," Kiyoko said. "She said she hires people who can't be replaced."

"She's a smart cookie." She hefted a book. The spine said *Quo Vadis?* "Jobs come and go. You don't. Ya savvy?"

"Yes," Kiyoko said.

Then, without warning, Belle turned and bellowed "Yo!" to a thin, chinless guy with too much gel in his hair. He looked thrilled, smiling shyly as he bent over a big cart overflowing with envelopes and retrieved a pile.

"That's the new mailroom guy, Kiyoko. Wherever you go, make friends with the mail guy, the photocopy guy, all those guys. When your neck is on the line, they'll help you out nine times out of ten."

Kiyoko mimicked writing a note to herself. Then she said, "Where's Shawn?"

"New assistant. Photography." She grinned. "A real go-getter."

"I'm glad for him," Kiyoko said sincerely.

Belle said, "I want you to stay in touch with me, okay? I'm valuable for you to know. And you can do me some good, too."

"I can?" Kiyoko asked, bewildered. *What on earth can I do for her?*

"Sure." Belle gave her a quick wink. "You're going places, Kiyoko. Never doubt that." She changed the subject. "Listen, I'm probably going to be in Tokyo around Christmas. Wanna hang?"

"Too bloody right," Kiyoko said eagerly. "No one celebrates Christmas quite the way we do."

Belle nodded. "I know. I'm at belle.holder@worldservice.com, good?"

"Yes," Kiyoko said.

She gave Kiyoko a wave and went back to her unpacking. "Stay good, Ki. You're a keeper."

And Kiyoko went back to Entertainment to finish out the day.

Matteo.

He and Kiyoko took a carriage ride through Central Park. It was hot, and they were wearing shorts. The sun was sinking, but night would do nothing to cool down the city.

But Kiyoko realized that she and Matteo had cooled down.

How?

When?

Saddened, she kept her head on his shoulder and pondered her feelings. She had never been where she was before. Matteo was her first boyfriend. She adored him. He was funny, warm, and darling. They had met in the cafeteria at the Tokyo International School, after he had slipped a chrysanthemum onto her desk. You didn't just summarily dump a guy like that.

They wound their way past the hot, dusty trees and the pond where kids were floating sailboats and over the bridle path and across a bridge.

Across a bridge.

He spent a lot of the ride telling her about USC. He was very excited about going. She loved that. She loved his smile and his American-ness.

But . . .

"When's your last day?" he asked. "Friday?"

"Thursday," she told him. "They wanted to give us a long weekend to enjoy the city before we left. There will be a lunch, and we'll get a certificate."

"Seems kind of lame after everything you've gone through. All those weeks, all that pressure."

"I got a music deal," she said, staring at the horizon as the sun splashed gold and orange behind the skyscrapers. "And some great friends."

There was a silence. Then Matteo said, "Yeah." He put his arms around her so that her head rested on his chest. "Tell me about your music. Don't leave out a single thing."

She did, working hard to share it with him. But it was a one-way street. It was like it still stayed with her; it didn't transfer to him. She tried to make him hear the beautiful cascades of music. Make him see Shinichiro Matsumoto and Jiro Kanno listening, enraptured, to something two kids had composed.

He listened, and he smiled, but when she was finished, it didn't have anything to do with him. Manga psychedelic belonged to her.

And . . . Cody?

☙ ☙ ☙ ☙

The lunch was held in the cafeteria. Each department head presented a certificate to his or her intern and talked about what an asset to the magazine she had been. Belle and Trey both stood with Kiyoko. People took pictures. The interns took pictures. Alexa took more than everyone else combined.

"See you on the network," Kiyoko told Trey.

She and her three mates took a last stroll through the halls of *Flirt* magazine.

"I feel like we just got here," Mel said. "Like I'm finally settled, and now I have to leave."

"I feel the same," Alexa said. "I didn't pull half the pranks I dreamed up." Her voice was wistful. "We had some crazy times, eh, amigas?"

"Sí," Liv murmured. "Crazy times."

"We'll have to stay in touch," Mel said.

"Absolutely," Kiyoko replied. But would they, really? It was hard to say.

☺   ☺   ☺   ☺

Then . . . their last night together.

Alexa, Mel, Kiyoko, and Liv decided to spend their last evening at Bowlmor. It was the first place the interns had gone together; now it would be the last. They arrived there at five thirty. After fifteen minutes or so, Nick Lyric joined them.

"My mom's home making you guys a cake," Nick told them while he poured the last of the Diet Coke into Mel's glass. "So let's not go back too late."

Kiyoko wondered if Nick was sorry that he had never hooked up with Mel. But he hadn't, and now Mel would return to Northern California, and write.

They were in the bar, hoping for a pitcher of hard lemonade eventually, but at the moment making do with every diet that contained caffeine. And several platters of tempura veggies.

Matteo arrived at six thirty, and Kiyoko felt a lump in her throat as he quietly came up beside her.

At about six forty-five, Matteo leaned in toward Kiyoko and said, "We need to talk."

She took a breath. The time had come.

Grasping his hand, she slid out of the booth, urging him along with her. She caught Mel's eye; her buddy mouthed, *"Good luck,"* and Kiyoko tipped her head a fraction of an inch in thanks.

As she prepared herself, he enfolded both her hands in his and said, "I wasn't out of line when I lost it that night. You were my girlfriend, and that guy was poaching." Then he leaned forward and kissed her nose. "I'm crazy about you, crazy girl. And I know you think I'm hot."

"I do," she said sincerely. She said nothing more. . . because there was nothing more to say.

The hurt on his face hurt her. His sadness was her sadness as well. And yet . . . she was very young. And so was he.

"So, maybe when you've taken the world on, we can try this again." Matteo waggled his brows.

> **She reached out her arms, and even though the Katsudas weren't big on hugging, she gave him a rib-cracking embrace, holding tight because she was letting go.**

She reached out her arms, and even though the Katsudas weren't big on hugging, she gave him a rib-cracking embrace, holding tight because she was letting go.

He deflated, sighing heavily and slowly, letting his head flop onto her shoulder. "We'll still text, right?"

"Of course. But if we start dating other people . . ." She took a breath. "*When* we start dating, maybe let's don't talk about it, okay? That would be bloody weird."

"With you there, Katsuda," he said.

They brushed lips. She felt a pang, but something shifted inside: a lightness. An intuition. This was the right thing to do.

In all honesty, there was relief mingled with the sadness.

He left. He had planned to spend more time with her in the city, but he'd changed his ticket to get back to California. That would make for a cleaner break than dragging around New York together in post-breakup mode.

Her three friends gathered around her, cheering and

comforting her. She would never have dreamed that she would feel so close to three such different girls. Another example of her fantastic karma.

By then it was seven, and Nick was pushing for them to go back to the loft. It seemed a little anticlimactic to return voluntarily while it was so early, but Kiyoko and her mates eventually caved. They cabbed it, Kiyoko staring out at all the scenery and Mel and Alexa insisted upon paying. Kiyoko understood that this was a statement of their own growing independence, so she signaled to Liv that they ought to let them.

Sammy was on duty in the lobby. He bowed to Kiyoko and said, "*Komban wa,* Katsuda-san. You will be late in one hundred and forty-eight minutes."

She bowed back and said, "About *Lost.* Sawyer is actually an alien. His race is conducting an experiment to see how humans behave during a crisis so they can decide whether or not to invade us."

He shook his head. "Don't even try."

"Kiyoko!" Melanie called from the open lift. Everyone was waiting.

"Un momento," she said, pointing a finger into the air. She reached into her purse and pulled out a small package wrapped in the pages of a manga book. "For you," she told Sammy.

"Oh." He raised his brows. "That's so sweet." He lowered his brows. "Right? It's something nice?"

"Something little." It was an English-Japanese

dictionary of "gutter slang, obscenities, and profanities."
She had had no idea there were so many words and phrases
in English to describe passing gas. She bowed again. "Thank
you for taking such good care of us."

He unwrapped his present—something a Japanese
man would never do in the presence of the person who
had given it to him—guffawed, and bowed a second time
as well. *"Arigato gozaimashita." Thank you very much.*

"Domo," she replied. *You're welcome.*

"Also, thank you for sneaking in the back way so
that I would not lose my job and wind up living in the
Dumpster."

She bowed a third time. No one could outbow a
Japanese person. "Honorable doorman, no one lives in the
Dumpster. Alexa and I would have met them long ago."

"You are as wily as you are witty," he said.

"I don't know what wily means."

He handed her the dictionary. "Look it up."

She pushed it back at him. "I bought an extra."

They smiled at each other. She wondered how old
he was. He was just adorable. And he obviously totally
wanted her.

Then she turned and dashed into the lift.

The party of five whooshed up to the twelfth floor.
Kiyoko heard a lot of noise through the loft entry door;
when Nick opened it with a flourish, a huge chorus of
voices cried, "Surprise!"

Gen and Charlotte stood with drink glasses beside

> **He unwrapped his present—something a Japanese man would never do in the presence of the person who had given it to him.**

their department heads. All the others were there, too, and Belle, Trey, and Quinn, and even Ms. Bishop. Ben and Eli had been invited, too. The entire loft had been transformed. A canopy of balloons gleamed below a mesh of tiny white lights. Enormous silver vases of red and white roses had been artfully arranged into pathways leading to a trio of food stations where chefs in white hats and coats were presiding over steak and French fries, sushi, and Indian food.

Nick put his arm loosely around Mel's shoulders and said, "I thought you guys would never leave that bowling alley!"

"We needed the time to finish getting ready anyway," Gen said. Beside her, Charlotte nodded.

Kiyoko went up to them and said, "This is bloody amazing."

"Even more amazing? I never, ever have to proofread copy about low-carb diets again."

Kiyoko wrinkled her nose. "Health and Fitness was the lamest beat."

They both laughed. Charlotte said, "Still, I'll have a *Flirt* internship listed on every single college application

I fill out. And I have a personalized exercise and beauty regimen created especially for me by the highly trained professionals at *Flirt.*" She flexed her biceps, and Kiyoko let out a whoop.

"Snap!" she cried. "You're a regular warrior woman!"

"And you should know, Anime Chick!" Charlotte said, laughing.

"I should." Kiyoko grinned at her.

Then she walked up to Ms. Bishop, who had been talking to Emma. Emma, with whom Kiyoko had made peace, moved away to give them privacy.

The grand lady turned to Kiyoko, one eye cocked.

"Belle told me that there was no way *Rolling Stone* would have ever attempted to publish my piece. You let me think so. It was kind."

Ms. Bishop gazed at her coolly. "Au contraire, Ms. Katsuda. I play poker with Jay Goldstein the first Friday of every month. I owe him a significant amount of money, and he told me he was willing to forgive the debt if I would let him have your article. So."

Sweet!

"We need a picture for our website," Alexa announced. "Our *good* website."

She hustled everyone over to the bright red couch, moving all the pillows to give everyone lots of room. Kiyoko felt a little odd around Lynn, but the photographer was all smiles as she said to Alexa, "Compose the shot, please."

"Everybody, squeeze in close. Big smiles," Alexa said. "Kiyoko, you sit next to Mel. I'll sit on your other side. Then Liv, Gen, Charlotte. The six interns!"

Alexa crowded in beside her, slinging her arm around Kiyoko. From her vantage point, Kiyoko could see the brilliant lights of New York at night. She remembered the night not so very long ago when she had felt like a bird in a cage.

Now the cage door is open, she thought. *I can hear my own heart singing. It's making music.*

KIYOKO'S BLOG:

Sim! Be bold! Take a chance!
Dream.

"On the count of three," Lynn said. "One, two . . ."

"Cheese!" everyone shouted.

Adeus, Flirt, Kiyoko thought, her eyes brimming. *Thank you for this grand adventure. And now . . .*

. . . May we see the world and charm many hearts.

Kaneland Middle School
1N137 Meredith Rd.
Maple Park, IL 60151